A crack in the front door opened and a man with a rifle shouted, "Who goes there sneakin' around in the dark!"

"I'm a friend of Miss Holden's. Who are you and what are you doing in that house? You're trespassing!"

There was a moment of silence, and then the man in the doorway swore and opened fire on Longarm. His first rifle bullet clipped the horn of Longarm's saddle, and the second bullet skinned the sorrel gelding's shoulder and sent it rearing over backward. The animal was hurt and wild with pain. It tore loose from Longarm's grasp, got up, and went galloping off into the night.

Longarm dropped to the ground where he was no longer a clear or easy target. He yanked out his six-gun and returned fire. The door slammed shut, and then two rifles busted windowpanes in the front of the house and belched flames.

Well, Longarm thought, *at least I've learned that there is more than one of them in the house . . .*

TABOR EVANS

LONGARM
AND LOVIN' LIZZY

JOVE BOOKS, NEW YORK

THE BERKLEY PUBLISHING GROUP
Published by the Penguin Group
Penguin Group (USA) Inc.
375 Hudson Street, New York, New York 10014, USA
Penguin Group (Canada), 90 Eglinton Avenue East, Suite 700, Toronto, Ontario M4P 2Y3, Canada
(a division of Pearson Penguin Canada Inc.)
Penguin Books Ltd., 80 Strand, London WC2R 0RL, England
Penguin Group Ireland, 25 St. Stephen's Green, Dublin 2, Ireland (a division of Penguin Books Ltd.)
Penguin Group (Australia), 250 Camberwell Road, Camberwell, Victoria 3124, Australia
(a division of Pearson Australia Group Pty. Ltd.)
Penguin Books India Pvt. Ltd., 11 Community Centre, Panchsheel Park, New Delhi—110 017, India
Penguin Group (NZ), 67 Apollo Drive, Rosedale, North Shore 0632, New Zealand
(a division of Pearson New Zealand Ltd.)
Penguin Books (South Africa) (Pty.) Ltd., 24 Sturdee Avenue, Rosebank, Johannesburg 2196,
South Africa

Penguin Books Ltd., Registered Offices: 80 Strand, London WC2R 0RL, England

This is a work of fiction. Names, characters, places, and incidents either are the product of the author's imagination or are used fictitiously, and any resemblance to actual persons, living or dead, business establishments, events, or locales is entirely coincidental.

LONGARM AND LOVIN' LIZZY

A Jove Book / published by arrangement with the author

PRINTING HISTORY
Jove edition / October 2008

ISBN: 978-0-515-14540-3

JOVE®
Jove Books are published by The Berkley Publishing Group,
a division of Penguin Group (USA) Inc.,
375 Hudson Street, New York, New York 10014.
JOVE is a registered trademark of Penguin Group (USA) Inc.
The "J" design is a trademark belonging to Penguin Group (USA) Inc.

PRINTED IN THE UNITED STATES OF AMERICA

10 9 8 7 6 5 4 3 2 1

Chapter 1

Deputy United States Marshal Custis Long was leaning forward into one of Denver's bitterest January snowstorms when he heard a faint cry for help. At first, he just thought it was the whistle of the hard wind through the tall buildings on Colfax Avenue, but then he realized it was a woman's desperate plea. Blundering forward into the wind with his hat pulled down low, Longarm tried to guess where the cry was coming from, but that was almost impossible.

He had just gotten off work at the Federal Building and was on his way to his rooms near Cherry Creek. At this hour, the sidewalks of downtown Denver should have been packed with other employees hurrying home, but because of the ferocity of the winter storm, the streets seemed eerily emptied. The storm had dropped three feet of snow in less than twenty-four hours and it showed no signs of letup. All horse-drawn wagons and carriages were gone and everyone in town was already hunkered down and expecting the worst that the weather could offer.

"Help!"

The voice was shrill and the cry swirled all around Longarm as he bulled his half-blinded way forward in a desperate search. He removed the glove from his right hand

and drew his often-used Colt .44-40 revolver. For a moment, he considered calling out to the victim, but then decided that might make things even worse, so he turned his ear away from the wind and listened hard.

"Help! Somebody, please help me!"

Longarm thought that the cry was coming from just ahead, and he leaned into the storm and charged forward. He tripped over a fire hydrant and slipped on the icy sidewalk, almost falling, but caught his balance and kept moving.

"There!" he said to himself as he saw three dark figures in the driving snow. The smaller of them was lying sprawled in a snowbank while the larger pair was leaning over what must have been the woman and were trying to unbutton her coat and remove something that Longarm assumed was the woman's purse.

Longarm did not offer the pair of muggers any warning, but instead raised the barrel of his pistol and slashed it down hard across one man's skull, sending him crashing face-first into the snowbank.

The second mugger swung around and charged Longarm with a short club in his left hand. Longarm could have shot the man, but instead he dodged the club and smashed the mugger across the face, busting his nose and opening up a huge gash. Blood gushed out across the man's face and he cried out in pain, but he did not go down. Instead, he stood half-blinded by both the storm and his own gore and began to wildly swing the club to fend Longarm off.

A patch of ice sent Longarm to the hard pavement, and he instinctively threw out his left arm to try and cushion his fall. His left elbow struck the ice and he felt a sharp pain shoot up his forearm. The attacker jumped on him and used his club as a bar in a desperate attempt to choke Longarm to death. The man was huge and he leaned forward with all his weight and power. Longarm felt a torrent of wet, warm blood wash across his own face as he struggled to throw the giant aside. But the wooden club was at his throat and pressing down so hard that Longarm could not breathe.

They were locked that way for what seemed like forever while Longarm frantically struggled to throw the man's weight off his chest and break the stranglehold. His gun had been knocked from his grasp and was buried somewhere in the snowbank. Longarm had a two-shot derringer cleverly attached to his watch fob and chain, but he couldn't get his hands on the little weapon and despite his own size and exceptional strength, Longarm felt as if he were being pushed down into an onrushing darkness from which there was no earthly return.

Suddenly and from far, far away, he heard the woman yell and her cry was immediately followed by gunshots. The giant on top of Longarm attempted to twist away, but two bullets sent into his massive skull exploded fragments of bone, brain matter, and even more blood all over Longarm. What had already been a ruined, bloody face now resembled nothing even remotely human.

The giant's back arched and his hands lifted skyward a moment before he pitched over backward twitching in death.

Longarm sucked in great lungfuls of air and with his chest heaving, he stared up at a young woman who was holding his six-gun in both hands and swaying against the hard wind. Then, as he tried to scramble to his feet, the young woman fainted onto the deep and bloodstained snow.

"Miss!" Longarm scrabbled to her side, retrieving and then holstering his Colt revolver. He brushed snow from the woman's face and saw that one of her eyes was swelling shut and that her lips were smashed to a pulp. "Miss, you have to wake up!"

Longarm grabbed a handful of snow and rubbed it on the woman's face, wiping away blood but was unable to

3

revive the victim. He saw that her skin was bone-white and realized that she was in her twenties, with dark hair, and that she would have been considered striking had it not been for the obvious beating that she'd just suffered.

The attacker that Longarm had pistol-whipped was moaning and starting to come around. With his hands full trying to take care of the young woman, Longarm had no time or pity for the reviving mugger. Normally, he would have arrested the thug and hauled him off to the local jail, but instead Longarm struck him a second time with the barrel of the Colt and sent him into a deep state of unconsciousness. Later, Longarm might try to come back and arrest the man if the mugger didn't first freeze to death beside the dead giant, that is. But Longarm didn't care one way or the other. Two criminals so vile that they would savagely attack and rob a lone young woman very much deserved to die.

Longarm looked around for someone to help, but the street was a total whiteout, so he found his flat-brimmed Stetson and replaced it on his head, pulling it down tight to keep from losing it in the strong, gusting wind. Then Longarm retrieved his revolver, bent down, and picked up the young woman. He was only a few blocks from his rooms, while the nearest doctor or hospital was beyond reach in this powerful storm.

Getting back to his rooms with the young woman in his arms was no small feat. The sidewalk was treacherous; the wind seemed always directly in his face. Longarm leaned into the blast and kept his head down as he staggered ahead, only looking up occasionally to find landmarks and get his bearings. It seemed to take him at least an hour to reach his building, but in reality it probably took less than fifteen minutes. When he came to the front door, he had to lay the unconscious woman in the snow in order to pry the door open. For a few frantic seconds, it was touch-and-go

4

whether or not he could get the door open and the woman and himself inside and out of the relentless storm.

Longarm somehow managed the feat, and the door slammed shut behind him. He was so accustomed to leaning forward that he almost pitched headfirst into the row of mailboxes in the tiny foyer.

"Sonofabitch, what a miserable storm!" he raged, picking up the woman and then staggering up a flight of creaking stairs to his rooms. Moments later, he had the door unlocked and slammed shut behind him. The rooms were small and chilly, but tidy. Longarm found a match and, shivering with cold and feeling his throat constricting from the near-strangulation he'd suffered, he lit his lamps and then turned on the heat that ducted up through the brick walls from a coal-fired furnace located in the building's brick-lined basement.

"Miss?" he croaked, carrying the unconscious lady to his sofa and laying her down gently. "Miss?"

She moaned, but did not revive.

Longarm found a wet washcloth and cleaned her battered face, then washed his hands and removed both of their cold and soggy coats. It was then that he noticed that the woman still clutched her purse in her nearly frozen hand.

"I'll say this much for you," Longarm told the unconscious woman. "Those two picked the wrong one to rob in a blinding snowstorm. You're either the grittiest girl in Denver, or you've got something in that purse that you consider to be more important than your life."

Longarm checked the woman's pulse and then studied her face. She was remarkably pretty, and he gritted his teeth in fury that two thugs would do this to someone so lovely and innocent.

"They beat the hell out of you, all right. But you shot the giant to death, and his friend that I pistol-whipped is most

5

likely already frozen, so I guess that it all worked out fine. In the morning, a constable on patrol will find both men dead and wonder what in the world could have happened to them. I'll have to file a report with the local authorities, but I won't do it until this storm has passed and you are awake and on the mend."

Longarm was numb and shaking from the cold, so he put on a pot of coffee to boil and found a bottle of whiskey with which he intended to lace the coffee to give it a little more fire.

"If you don't mind, I could sure use a taste of that bottle," the young woman said in a soft and slightly slurred voice. "But again, only if you don't mind."

Longarm had just taken a deep swig from the bottle, and was enjoying the whiskey heat as it made its way down his gullet to his gut. At the sound of the woman's voice, he looked up and smiled at her with reassurance.

"You're going to be all right, miss."

"I certainly hope so after all that I went through out there in the storm." She opened her purse, counted money, and then closed the purse again. "Are you my knight in shining armor?"

"No, I'm just a poorly paid federal marshal who was lucky enough to be able to come to your assistance."

"What happened to those . . . animals?"

Longarm came over and placed the bottle of whiskey in her hands. "You don't remember?"

"No," she replied, taking a deep pull on the bottle and shuddering as the liquor went down hard. "I don't remember much of anything after the big one hit me in the face and knocked me down in a snowbank. I do remember struggling and trying to hang on to my purse. And . . . and I think that I cried out for help."

"Yes," Longarm said, "you cried out and I heard you as I was coming home from the office. There wasn't anyone else nearby because of the storm."

6

She took another drink and handed the bottle back to him with tears in her brown eyes. "Did they get away free?"

"No," Longarm told her. "They're both dead and probably already covered by snow and getting stiff as boards."

"But how . . ."

"I pistol-whipped one hard enough to kill him," Longarm said. "The other man took two bullets from my gun to his brain . . . What little there might have been before was soon plastered all over the fresh snow."

She shuddered, clearly rattled. "You brained one and shot the other to death?"

Longarm hesitated before answering. It was obvious that this woman did not remember shooting the giant twice in the back of his head. So it seemed to Longarm that it would be much easier to tell the local law officials that he had killed *both* muggers. There would be few if any questions from the authorities, and it would be understood that Longarm had done the city a good public service. However, if it were learned that the young woman had actually been the one to shoot the giant to death, then things would get much stickier and more complicated. The young woman might even have to go to trial and face a barrage of distasteful questions.

"Yes," Longarm fibbed, "I shot the big one to death. He was strangling me with a club and I was fortunate to get out from under him and find my gun in the snow."

"I can see a dark bruise on your throat," she said with a look of sudden concern. "I'm so very sorry that you had to be hurt."

"I'll mend fast."

"So will I." The woman tried to sit up. "I should be going now. I've imposed enough on you for one day."

"Not at all," he told her. "The storm outside hasn't let up even a bit. You'd lose your way and maybe die of exposure out there."

7

"I am pretty tough," she replied, raising her chin.

"I know you are," he said, "but all the same, I'd like to think that my efforts today weren't wasted and that you came out of this safe and sound."

She smiled, and it caused her to wince with pain. "What is your name . . . or should I just call you Sir Galahad?"

"Custis," he said. "Deputy U.S. Marshal Custis Long."

"I am so very pleased to meet you, Custis, and also beyond grateful for your heroics out there on Colfax during that terrible storm. I had the feeling that after those thieves got my purse, they would have clubbed me to death or left me lying unconscious in the snow to freeze."

"I expect that they might have," Longarm agreed. "I've seen them a time or two on the streets before and have always felt they were dangerous. But not anymore."

"No," she said quietly, "not anymore."

"What is your name and who are you?" he asked.

"My name is Elizabeth, but everyone calls me Lizzy. Lizzy Holden."

Longarm wanted to know more. "Are you married with children?"

"No, are you?"

Longarm shook his head. "Come close a time or two, but I'd be a poor husband since I travel so much and my profession involves danger."

Lizzy studied him closely. "I'm absolutely sure that you'd be worth worrying about, Custis."

"That's debatable," he said, blushing with her compliment. "Care for another drink? I've got coffee started and I like to lace it with whiskey when it's so cold in these rooms."

"I'd really like some coffee laced with your whiskey," she told him. "But even more, I'd like to use the bathroom to clean up a little."

"Down the hallway to the left. It's at the end."

"Are you sure that there are no muggers lurking in the building?" she asked, almost teasing.

"I'm sure. You see, I've long ago either run 'em off or killed 'em, Miss Holden."

Her laughter was contagious and it lifted Longarm's spirits. His rooms were warming up and he had plenty of food in his icebox . . . enough to carry them through the night if need be and well into tomorrow. *Who knows*, he thought, *maybe this storm is a good thing after all, and I'll get lucky tonight with the brave and beautiful Miss Lizzy Holden.*

Chapter 2

Lizzy yawned, hiccupped, and finally asked, "Is that clock on your mantel right? Is it really nine o'clock already?"

Longarm drained his bottle of excellent Kentucky whiskey into both their coffee cups, which had long since held no coffee. "Nope," he told her, checking out his pocket watch. "That old clock hasn't worked for years. It's really eleven thirty."

"My, oh, my," Lizzy exclaimed with a titter, "time really flies when you're having fun."

"It does," Longarm said, glancing toward his small bedroom. "But the storm outside is still howling and I'm getting sleepy. Maybe it's time to go to bed."

She giggled, clearly beyond being just tipsy. "Are you hinting that we ought to *both* go to your bed?"

"The idea has occurred to me," he admitted.

"Yeah, I'll bet it has! You've been eyeballing me from head to toe for the last few hours. You have the look of a hungry wolf, Marshal."

He sipped some more whiskey. "Is that a fact?"

"It is."

"Well," he told her, "even beaten up, you are a beautiful woman, and it is going to be a long, cold night."

11

"I owe you," she said, looking him right in the eye. "I owe you everything I have left to offer."

"No, you don't," he countered. "You don't owe me a thing. And if you want to sleep on that couch that you're sitting on, that's perfectly fine with me. But I'm going to bed."

He started to climb to his feet, but her words stopped him. "Custis, do you want to know how much money they would have taken from me if you hadn't stopped them?"

Longarm shook his head. "That's your business, Lizzy. The only thing I needed to know was that they were criminals and they deserved what happened to them out in that storm."

"I have just over three thousand dollars in my purse," she blurted. "Other than a small cattle ranch in the Rockies, all my saved money is right here in my purse."

"Well," Longarm jokingly told her, "that's about three thousand more dollars than I have saved."

Lizzy didn't laugh at his attempt at humor. "This money is from the sale of my father's cattle and horses. My father was murdered last month up in the Rockies."

Longarm didn't bother to hide his surprise. "Murdered?"

"Yes."

"How and why?"

Lizzy looked away quickly, then dried fresh tears in her eyes. "I can't answer those questions," she told him. "My mother died four years ago and my father was a rancher and part-time prospector. I think that he found gold somewhere up near the ranch and that he must have told someone who told someone bad."

Longarm sat back down and looked at the girl. "You think that your father was murdered for gold?"

"Yes."

"But you don't know where the gold was found . . . or even for sure if it was found."

"That's right." Lizzy drank more of his Kentucky

whiskey. "I was living in St. Louis when word came of my father's untimely death. It was just a telegram from a neighboring rancher and there were no details. Nothing like you'd expect. It didn't say that my father died of a sudden and unexpected heart failure. Or an accident on the ranch involving a horse or a piece of equipment. Just that he had died and that he was buried by friends and neighbors beside my dear mother."

Longarm frowned. "What were you doing in St. Louis, if you don't mind my asking?"

"I don't. I was engaged to be married to a prominent and very successful surgeon. But even before the letter arrived, I'd about decided to break off the engagement. My fiancé, Dr. Bernard Kingsley, was kind, very wealthy, and the best catch in town, but I didn't love him. Not enough to want to marry him and have his children. And besides, I didn't fit into the high society of St. Louis, and I couldn't fake it with those other envious women."

"So you were coming home even before you learned of your father's death?"

"Yes. Father and I were very close, and he needed my help. I'd . . ."

She hesitated and couldn't continue.

"Lizzy, you don't have to tell me your life story," Longarm said. "In the first place, it's none of my business. In the second place, I can see that it's painful for you."

"I was in love with a young cowboy who worked on our ranch. Without planning to, I got pregnant and was going to have a baby by him . . . but of course that would have been scandalous, so I went to St. Louis to have the baby and give it up for adoption. Bernard was the doctor who delivered the baby. He was immediately attracted to me despite my sad and tawdry circumstances. He urged me to give the child up and then start a new life and marry him."

"It sounds like a very nice solution to a bad problem you had."

13

"I know. But I didn't love him. I still loved my young cowboy, but I did give the baby up for adoption as Bernard insisted. I've regretted it every minute since."

"So what happened to the cowboy you loved?"

"He got in a poker game and was shot to death in Durango. My father didn't give me all the details, but I was devastated and in my grief I finally agreed to marry Bernard. We were engaged for over a year. His parents, rich and influential, hated and looked down on me with unconcealed contempt. I couldn't stand either one of them and told that to Bernard."

Longarm found another bottle of whiskey and poured a generous dollop for each of them. "So what did your doctor fiancé say when you told him you and his parents would never be friends?"

"He offered to move us to New York City," Lizzy said. "He would have done anything to keep me. He was that much in love."

Longarm sipped his whiskey, lost in thought for several minutes. "This doctor doesn't sound like a bad man to marry."

"He would have been a wonderful husband . . . except for one very important thing."

"That being?"

"He loved me, but he also loved the company of men."

"Not unusual," Longarm said with a shrug of his broad shoulders.

Lizzy was silent for a moment, then looked up and said, "Bernard's . . . uh, physical relationships with men were, sadly, *very* unusual."

Longarm swallowed and looked away for a moment to compose his reaction. "Oh. I see."

"Bernard couldn't seem to help himself, but I couldn't bear the thought of him and some man . . . well, you understand, don't you?"

14

"I sure as hell do," Longarm told her. "But let's get back to your father and his supposed murder."

"It was not 'supposed.' I talked to the local doctor, who was a longtime friend of my father. He said Father was shot in the back by a high-powered rifle. They didn't find his body for almost a week and by then it was . . ."

Lizzy couldn't finish, and burst into tears.

Longarm came to her side and put his arm around her. "I'm sorry," he said. "I don't think you should talk about it anymore. At least not with me and not tonight."

Her head snapped up. "But I have to! Do you know why I am carrying three thousand dollars in cash?"

"No."

"I came to Denver to find a private detective. One that would not only find out who murdered my father, but also a man that would *kill* the murderer. You see, Custis, I wanted revenge no matter what the cost."

Longarm stepped back and asked the obvious question. "Did you have any luck finding such a man?"

"I did," Lizzy replied. "I asked all around Denver . . . which wasn't an easy or comfortable thing to do."

"I wouldn't think so."

"And I was given the same name by several different people who were pretty rough."

"Mind telling me who they referred you to?" Longarm asked.

"A man named Joe Bean."

Lizzy saw Longarm blink with surprise. "I can tell that you've heard of Mr. Bean."

"I've not only heard of him," Longarm said, "I once worked with Joe, and then later arrested and sent him to prison for murder."

For a moment, they both stared, and then Lizzy said, "Is Mr. Bean . . . good at his work?"

"He's better than good," Longarm replied. "Joe Bean is

an ex-lawman. He's a professional bounty hunter and assassin. He's as dangerous and cunning as any man that I've ever known. I learned some things from him that I'll never forget and that have served me well on my own manhunts."

"Good!"

"Not good," Longarm countered. "Joe Bean is not to be trusted. He'll kill anyone to produce a body, and then he'll tell you that he brought you justice and demand that you pay him in full."

Lizzy looked down at the purse in her lap and fidgeted nervously. "But . . . but surely he wouldn't really kill an innocent person and claim that person to be my father's murderer!"

"Oh, yes, he would," Longarm countered. "Did you already pay Joe Bean an advance against his expenses?"

"Of course. I paid him a thousand dollars. I agreed to pay him another thousand when the job was done."

Longarm groaned.

Lizzy drained her whiskey and raised her chin. "I guess I've done a terrible thing, haven't I?"

"Let's just say that you made a bad but understandable mistake."

"Then I'll look up Mr. Bean tomorrow and ask for my money back and tell him our arrangement is finished."

"You won't find him," Longarm told her. "And if you did, Joe Bean would look you in the eye and then kill you for that three thousand you have in your purse. For all I know, he might have hired those two muggers to do the work for him."

"No!"

"Oh, yes," Longarm said with conviction. "Joe Bean would do that in a heartbeat."

"But why would he trust two men like that to bring him my purse with all that money?"

"Because they would know that Joe Bean would not only find and kill them, but he'd torture them in ways that you can't even imagine."

Lizzy groaned and shook her head. "I've really gotten myself in a pickle, haven't I?"

"I'm afraid so," Longarm told her. "Not only did you pick the wrong man to find out who murdered your father, but you put a killer on your own tail and he won't stop until he has the rest of your money."

"But what if I put this three thousand in a bank's safe-deposit box and . . ."

"He'd kidnap and torture you until you retrieved the money and gave it to him, and then he'd kill you after he had his sick sexual pleasure."

Lizzy paled. "Is he that much of monster?"

"He is," Longarm said. "He's the sickest and most deadly man I know."

"Oh, God," she whispered, clapping her hands to the sides of her face. "What have I done!"

Longarm hugged her close. "What you did was make an honest mistake, Lizzy."

"One that was born of vengeance."

"Yes," Longarm agreed, "that's true. But now your most immediate problem isn't finding out who murdered your father and why . . . but how you get Joe Bean out of the picture."

"What would you suggest?"

Longarm looked away for a moment. "If I weren't a lawman, I'd suggest figuring out how to kill Joe Bean before he kills you for that money."

"But you *are* a lawman."

"That's right," he admitted. "And so I can't kill Joe Bean unless he kills you."

Lizzy swallowed hard. "I'm in a terrible mess. What on earth can I do!"

"Nothing for now," he told her. "We'll have to think on this some and come up with a plan to save your life."

"I want to cry," Lizzy said, biting her lower lip. "So much has gone wrong today that my head is spinning. I've been beaten up and now I see that I foolishly set myself up to be murdered."

"There's always a way out of bad situations, if you don't panic and use your wits and skills," Longarm said with conviction.

"Will you help me . . . again?"

Longarm stood up and headed for his bedroom, saying, "Sure I will, Lizzy. I'm your knight in shining armor. Right?"

"Right," she said, following him. "But you also carry a shining tin star."

"I'll work it out," he promised.

"I'll help you work it out," she pledged, peeling off her outer garments and following him into the bedroom. "Starting *tonight*."

"Sounds like a good start," he said with a wolfish grin.

They tumbled into bed beside a flickering candle while the wind howled outside and the snow came down blinding and fast. Longarm was extremely gentle when he kissed Lizzy's swollen and battered lips, and she kissed his bruised and painful throat where the giant had tried to strangle him on the icy sidewalk. Then Longarm kissed Lizzy's breasts until she moaned with pleasure. His tongue slipped down her flat stomach into the sweet secret of her silkiness, and she gasped and pressed his face deep into herself.

Longarm was a little drunk, but he was also patient and a lover that no woman ever forgot . . . ever. His tongue tasted Lizzy until her fingernails clawed at his back and she whimpered and groaned, begged and pleaded for him to take her deeply.

"Now, please," she panted, pulling him up and taking him into herself with an urgency that could not be denied. "More! Harder!"

Longarm's hips thrust like powerful pistons and he moved his manhood in an ellipse, giving them both full pleasure. He did not stop pumping her slick wetness until Lizzy cried out and her body began to shudder with a pounding violence that brought Longarm to a climax. With a growl from down deep inside, he filled her with torrents of his spewing hot seed.

At last, when they lay gasping and catching their breath, Lizzy wrapped a long leg across Longarm's back, then gently sucked on his earlobe until he laughed and turned to face her again.

"Custis, you were magnificent!"

"As good as your doctor in St. Louis?"

She scoffed. "Bernard was all method and technique and no passion whatsoever. Once, he actually timed himself, and was so proud that he lasted eighteen minutes in me before he found his full release."

"Eighteen minutes isn't bad, Lizzy."

She poked him in the side. "Don't tease. Bernard was a sweet man, but he was always thinking. Custis, don't take this as an insult, but you aren't such a sweet man. You're a good and brave man and you go way beyond thinking when you make love to a woman."

"Is that a fact?"

"It is most definitely," Lizzy assured him. "And I like your lovemaking far, far better than Bernard's."

"Well," Longarm told her, "I may not be as cerebral as your ex-fiancé, but I'd better start thinking hard tomorrow about how to handle Joe Bean."

"He won't know where I am," she said. "And more to the point, there was no way that he could have found out what happened today to his henchmen in that storm."

"He'll find out soon enough that they are both dead," Longarm promised. "And then he'll make it his mission in life to discover how they died when they should have robbed and murdered you."

Lizzy looked confused. "But . . . but *how* could he find out?"

19

"There are ways," Longarm said vaguely. "Does Joe Bean know where you live?"

"I . . . I'm afraid so."

"You rented a room somewhere, didn't you?"

"Yes."

"Then he'll go there tomorrow."

"It's a woman's boardinghouse," Lizzy explained. "Men aren't allowed inside."

"Joe Bean will make himself a notable exception . . . one way or the other. He'll be looking for clues among your belongings in that room. Anything to give him a lead on where you can be found."

"I see," she said, looking afraid. "And then he'll come to rob and kill me."

"That's right," Longarm said. "But starting tomorrow, I'll be waiting for him at the boardinghouse where you were staying here in Denver. I'll have a talk with him and get back your money."

"I don't think I want you to do that," Lizzy said, hugging Longarm tightly. "I think I'd much rather that you stayed away from Mr. Bean and not risk being killed."

Longarm smiled, but not with pleasure or mirth. "Lizzy, there isn't anything I can do to stop Joe Bean short of killing him or sending him to prison for years. And since I don't have any legitimate evidence that he sent those two muggers, I can't even arrest the man."

"Then what can you do?"

"I can have a real heart-to-heart talk with Joe Bean. I can tell him that I'll kill him if he doesn't give me back your money and give up the case."

"And if he refuses?"

Longarm leaned over and kissed her nipples, and then he ran a finger down through her wetness until she shivered with pleasure. "Then, Lizzy, I'll just have to do what comes natural to me."

"And kill him?"

"Maybe. He deserves to die. He's a very evil man."

Lizzy pressed his hand down hard so that Longarm's probing forefinger slid deeper into her wet womanhood. "Why don't we talk about Mr. Bean tomorrow and talk about us making love right now."

"We just made love."

"Yeah, but do me again, if you can."

He threw back his head and laughed even though it hurt his injured throat. Then Longarm began to stroke Lizzy into arousal while she spread her lovely legs wider and waited for him to mount her like a big, wild stallion.

Chapter 3

Mrs. Clara Waite ran The Pines, a very respectable boardinghouse for ladies on Welton Street, which was lined with stately poplar trees and well-kept Victorian homes. Longarm had visited The Pines on a few occasions when he'd met ladies in the parlor under Mrs. Waite's supervision and then escorted them to one social function or another before taking them to his rooms to make love. He suspected that Mrs. Waite did not especially like him, and most certainly did not trust him with her "ladies," but Longarm really didn't care what the stiff-necked old landlady thought.

Still, he knew that he was going to be in for a difficult session when he arrived at The Pines, so he asked Lizzy to write him a small note of introduction explaining that he needed to be there when Joe Bean came calling later.

"This note won't do a thing to help you get into that boardinghouse," Lizzy said, folding the short missive and then handing it to him. "Mrs. Waite is very set in her ways and unbending in her rules. No men allowed except in the parlor and then only by invitation."

"Well," Longarm said, patting the note he'd placed in

his coat pocket, "this note is my introduction. And as for Mrs. Waite, she'll just have to bend her rules."

Lizzy nodded, but did not look confident. "When you see Mr. Bean, tell him that I had a change of heart about hiring him to find my father's murderer."

"You may have had a change of heart," Longarm told her, "but Joe Bean will not see it that way, and he most certainly will be unwilling to return that thousand-dollar advance that you gave him."

Lizzy put her arm around his neck. "Custis, I really wish that you would just forget about Mr. Bean. A thousand dollars is a mountain of money to me, but it's not worth you risking your life to recover."

"I know," he told her. "But the truth of the matter is that I'm quite certain now that Joe Bean hired those two muggers who beat and nearly killed you yesterday."

"But you have no proof of that, and I'm sure that Mr. Bean would not admit to that fact."

"Of course he wouldn't," Longarm told her. "But all the same, I want to retrieve your money and tell Joe that he is walking on very thin ice with me and that he had better not try to give you any more trouble or I'll damn sure take it personally."

Lizzy stepped back. "He might lose his temper when you threaten him and try to kill you right in the parlor of that boardinghouse."

"If he does, you can rest assured that I'll be ready and able to deal with Joe once and for all," Longarm solemnly promised as he pulled on his heaviest coat and left his rooms and the anxious young woman.

Yesterday's fierce blizzard had finally abated, but snow was still falling lightly. The downtown streets were beautiful and deeply covered with fresh snow. Street cleaners were out in force, trying to clear the way so that commerce could resume. Pedestrians trod carefully on icy sidewalks, but they seemed happy to be outdoors on such a fine morning after such a ferocious winter storm.

Longarm arrived at The Pines shortly before eleven o'clock, dusted snow from his boots and coat, and removed his flat-brimmed hat before knocking on the door.

As expected, Mrs. Waite came to the door at once and asked him the nature of his business.

"I have a note from Miss Elizabeth Holden, who I believe is one of your guests. When you read the note, you will understand why I need to remain here until another man named Joe Bean arrives."

Mrs. Waite reached around the door and snatched the note from Longarm. She read it in a flash and then handed it back, saying, "I have no way of knowing who wrote that note, sir. Therefore, you cannot be allowed in my boardinghouse."

Longarm had anticipated the refusal, and he was already pushing the door and the landlady gently aside as he entered the parlor.

"Sir! How dare you barge in here uninvited!"

"I'm sorry," he told her, extracting his badge and showing it to the outraged woman. "But I am a deputy United States marshal and this is not a social call."

"It isn't?"

"No, ma'am. It's an official visit. I have reason to believe that Joe Bean was behind the deaths of two men yesterday."

"And what has that to do with Miss Holden or this establishment?" the sharp-featured woman in her sixties demanded.

"Mr. Bean might have hired the two men who were killed. I need to question him and I have every reason to believe he will come calling for Miss Holden this morning."

Mrs. Waite stomped her foot and folded her arms over her flat chest. "Marshal, you must wait outside."

"Your porch is covered with snow, Mrs. Waite. Further-more, it is still quite cold outside . . . in case you haven't noticed."

"Don't be impertinent with me, young man! I don't care if you have ten silver badges. This is a respectable establishment and I do not want trouble to sully its sterling reputation."

"I'll not cause you any trouble," Longarm promised, though he thought he might have to shoot Joe Bean in her parlor, which would certainly "sully" the sterling reputation of her ladies' boardinghouse.

"You will not leave at my request?"

"No, ma'am. And I wish to remain concealed in your parlor as long as possible. You see, I need the element of surprise when Mr. Bean arrives."

"This is highly outrageous and uncalled for!" the woman cried, shaking a bony fist in Longarm's face.

"I am sorry for the . . . the difficulty this creates for you, Mrs. Waite. However, it is absolutely essential that I remain here in your parlor and that you do nothing to alert Mr. Bean when he arrives. I need him to enter this parlor completely unaware that I am here waiting."

"And if I refuse to do that?"

"Then I might have to shoot Joe Bean dead on your porch, and that would mean that he would fall in a pool of blood and every neighbor on the street would come rushing over here to stare, and then they would gossip about this establishment for years."

Mrs. Waite paled at the thought, and finally nodded her head. "Very well, Marshal, you give me no choice but to agree to your demands. However, you must agree to one condition."

"And that is?"

"You will not, under any circumstances, create a disturbance in my parlor or damage my expensive furniture. And you most certainly must not kill Mr. Bean here. If you

26

absolutely must punch his ticket, take him up the street and when he is out of hearing distance, then you can shoot him full of holes for all that I care."

"Mrs. Waite, I . . ."

"It's that or I won't cooperate and the moment I see Mr. Bean on the sidewalk, I'll yell a warning to him that you are inside waiting to either arrest or kill him."

It was all that Longarm could do to curb his irritation and say, "All right, Mrs. Waite. I agree to your terms. No fighting or making a scene in your lovely parlor and no shooting the man on your property."

"Or on the street in front of this house! Good Lord, Marshal, my business and livelihood depend on my boarders trusting that this is a safe boardinghouse in a safe and peaceful neighborhood!"

"I understand."

"I very much doubt that," Mrs. Waite grumped. "But I will cooperate."

Longarm stepped into the parlor, which was large and overfilled with dark, heavy furniture. There were four couches and three chairs, all of them finely upholstered in pink silk with white flower patterns. Books, French lamps, and a chandelier that was probably worth a small fortune adorned the parlor, as did a magnificent Persian rug that was starting to become a bit threadbare.

"I will sit in that chair after I move it to the dimmest part of the room," Longarm told the landlady. "With your permission, of course."

"You do not have my permission, Marshal! That chair was imported from London, England, and it will not be moved under any circumstances!"

"Sorry," Longarm replied, moving the heavy chair to the dimmest corner in the room where he would not be immediately seen or recognized by Joe Bean.

"You are no gentleman!" Mrs. Waite stormed. "And I do not approve of you at all! I remember you coming here a

27

few times in the past to escort some of my ladies to this or that social occasion. And you never brought them home on time according to my rules, and when they did return they looked . . ."

"Happy?" Longarm said, tweaking the old monster.

"No! They looked dazed and disheveled."

"That's good to know," he said rather proudly. "Mrs. Waite, truth be told, your 'ladies' aren't always so ladylike after they leave your home."

Her pointy jaw dropped as the implication of what Longarm was saying sank home, and then she clamped it shut like a bear trap a moment before she marched out of the room in a fit of high anger.

Longarm nearly laughed. Would have laughed had it not been for the prospect of soon meeting Joe Bean under the absolute worst of circumstances.

Chapter 4

After all the intense lovemaking with Lizzy, Longarm was exhausted, and he must have drifted off to sleep in Mrs. Waite's easy chair because he was startled by the loud knock at her front door.

Mrs. Waite came down the stairs from her room, silent and quick as a snake. She peered into the corner where Longarm was rubbing his eyes and said, "Marshal, you've been dozing for almost two hours! If this is Mr. Bean, must I still let him inside this house?"

"Yes," Longarm said, sitting up straight and instantly alert.

"But no fighting or trouble!"

"No fighting or trouble," Longarm promised. "Open the door, Mrs. Waite. If he asks for Miss Holden, simply bring him inside, then leave at once. Allow none of your other boarders to come down the stairs until we are finished with our business."

"Very well, but I don't like you and I don't approve of this one little bit!"

"It won't be a very long meeting," Longarm told her. "It will all be over in just a few minutes, and then both Joe Bean and myself will be gone."

"Thank heavens, and never come back."

"I won't," Longarm told her.

As the pounding on her front door grew more insistent, the old woman opened the door a crack and said, "Yes?"

"I've come to visit Miss Elizabeth Holden. I understand that she is one of your boarders."

"She is one of my *guests*, sir. What is your name?"

"Joe Bean, ma'am."

Longarm didn't need to hear the man's name. He recognized the voice. Bean was now in his forties, but he had that deep and distinctively gravelly voice from years of heavy smoking. Bean wasn't a big man, but he stood almost six feet tall and was deceptively strong and quick. More than once in the early years, Longarm had seen Joe whip men far bigger and stronger than himself, and he knew Bean to be a vicious fighter who neither showed nor expected any quarter. Bean was also quick-tempered and dangerously unpredictable.

Mrs. Waite opened the door wide and led Joe into the parlor, then vanished like a ghost. Joe, his eyes accustomed to more light, did not see Longarm until he heard a familiar "Hello, Joe."

Bean's hand dropped to the gun on his hip, but Longarm had anticipated the move and already had his Colt up and leveled at Bean's chest. "I wouldn't advise you doing that."

Joe's hand froze an inch above the handle of his gun; then his long fingers twitched and relaxed as he moved his hand away from his weapon. "My, oh, my, if it isn't my old friend and fellow marshal Custis Long! What a surprise."

"Is it?" Longarm asked.

"Of course! Don't tell me that we're both here to see the same lovely young lady."

"No, we aren't," Longarm replied. "Because she's not here. I came to wait for *you*."

He feigned surprise. "Why, whatever for?"

30

"Why don't you keep your hands out in the open where I can see them and take a seat on one of Mrs. Waite's couches," Longarm suggested. "Then we can have a nice, pleasant conversation."

Bean looked around the room. "Pretty fancy place, huh, Custis. Sorta reminds me of the better grade of whorehouses we used to frequent."

"I never went to them," Longarm said. "Never paid a woman for pleasure in my life. You must have me confused with someone else from your past, Joe."

"Ah, I think you're right," Bean said with an oily smile. "You were always the gentleman . . . except when it came to humping all the ladies and killing outlaws."

"Always people that deserved killing, Joe."

"Maybe we *all* deserve being killed," Joe said with an innocent shrug of his shoulders. "At any rate, what do you want to talk about? Our storied past? Or perhaps our very interesting future?"

"Let's forget the past and talk about the future," Longarm said, keeping his Colt loosely pointed in Joe Bean's direction. "Let's talk about the one thousand dollars that Miss Holden gave you to find and eliminate the man who murdered her father."

"But that happened in the past," Joe said, managing to look confused. "I thought you wanted to talk about the future."

"All right. The future and the present. First off, Joe, I want that thousand dollars back right now for Miss Holden."

"Oh, you do, do you?" Joe asked, a hint of anger creeping into his voice. "And what if I told you that I have already spent it on this assignment that I was given by Miss Holden?"

"I'd say that was unlikely," Longarm told him. "How did you spend that much money so fast?"

"Oh, you know," Joe told him. "It is expensive to buy good help these days and you have to grease a lot of palms to get reliable information."

"This expensive help that you're referring to," Longarm said. "Would that be in the nature of two thugs . . . one of them a giant . . . who brutally attacked Miss Holden yesterday evening in the middle of the blizzard and tried to steal her purse while they knocked her senseless?"

Joe threw up his hands and looked offended. "Why, Marshal Long, whatever are you talking about?"

"I'm talking about the two thieves that attacked Lizzy and that I killed yesterday over on Colfax Avenue."

"You did? Nice work!"

Longarm shook his head. "Joe, you always were the smoothest liar I ever knew."

"I'll take that as a compliment, fortunate for you, Custis."

"So you hired that pair and you probably paid them ten or twenty dollars each, which is small change considering that they died badly."

"Custis, to be honest, I don't know what in the hell you're talking about."

"I want that thousand dollars back, Joe."

"Like I told you. I've already spent the money on the case. Sorry."

Longarm wanted to get up and shake the living shit out of Joe Bean, but that would not only be foolish but dangerous, so he said, "Joe, I can't arrest you without proof that you hired those thugs and since they're both dead, that proof isn't likely to ever materialize."

"I'm glad you see that so clearly. And that the thousand dollars I accepted has been spent as it was supposed to be spent."

Longarm knew that he held a losing hand in this argument. "Did you find out who killed Mr. Holden up near Salida?"

"Unfortunately, I did not. I have a few leads, however."

"Is that a fact?"

"It is," Joe said. "You must remember that I was a good

investigator. I taught you a lot of tricks when you were green and vulnerable to lies."

"Share your leads with me."

Joe Bean shook his head. "I don't think I want to do that, Custis. And I don't think you can make me tell you a damned thing."

"All right," Longarm said after curbing his rising anger. "You've got me over a barrel. But I want to tell you this. Miss Holden is dismissing you and from this time on, you will have no part in investigating what happened to her father."

Quickly and smoothly changing the subject, Joe said, "I heard that the old rancher struck gold. In fact, I knew about that before his daughter even came to me. Quite a coincidence, wouldn't you say? But so far, no one has found the location of the gold. Do you think it might be on his ranch . . . now his daughter's ranch? I swear, it has given me a touch of gold fever!"

"Did your gold fever lead you to kill Mr. Holden?" Longarm asked.

Bean smiled faintly. "It has kindled an interest in ranching."

"Joe, you're not listening," Longarm told the man. "You're out of this, and if I see you anywhere near that ranch or near Miss Holden, then I'll shoot you down like the mad dog you are."

For a moment, something terrible to behold passed across Joe Bean's pale gray eyes, and then it vanished. With an immense and visible effort, Bean composed himself and said, "The last I heard, this is still a free country, Custis. If you're telling me that I can't go poking around up near Salida like all the others who are looking for that lost gold strike, then I'd have to tell you to go straight to hell."

Longarm came to his feet and walked over to Joe, who also stood tense as a coiled steel spring. For a moment, they went eyeball to eyeball, and then Longarm hissed, "Stay away from Miss Holden and her ranch, Joe. If you don't, I will kill you without blinking an eye."

"If I don't kill you first," Joe whispered. "But tell me, Marshal, how is it that a man sworn to uphold the law intends to break the law?"

"Don't push me, Joe."

"But you just promised to shoot me on sight. How can you do that if you are a lawfully sworn lawman? Has something changed since I wore a badge?"

"Yeah, our law profession got a whole lot cleaner when you were stripped of your badge."

Joe paled and shuddered.

"Go ahead," Longarm said. "Reach for your gun."

Joe suddenly smiled. "You'd like that very much."

"I would."

"But you have your gun in your hand while mine is still in my holster. Doesn't seem fair somehow, does it?"

"Fair has never been in your vocabulary, Joe."

"Custis, I won't accommodate your wishes and foolishly be goaded into drawing my gun. So I'll be leaving now. Would you please give the lovely Miss Holden my regards and tell her that I really did not spend her one thousand dollars in vain. Tell her that I have spent it well and that she . . . she constantly remains in my thoughts."

"Get out of here, Joe. Get out before I put a bullet in your lying black heart and make a lifetime enemy of Mrs. Waite by ruining her Persian rug."

Joe Bean grinned. He had good, white teeth, and anyone who didn't know him well would have admired his deadly smile. Longarm knew it was a smile that said he intended to kill you sooner rather than later.

"See you around, Custis. Probably up around Salida, when the snow melts."

"I expect I'll see you long before that, Joe."

"You ever have gold fever?"

Longarm shook his head. "Can't say as I have."

"It's a strange thing that. Makes a man do things he never would have thought he'd do."

"Nothing you do would surprise me, Joe."

Bean chuckled at that remark and strolled out the door. He stopped and turned back to say, "Was a hell of a storm yesterday, wasn't it? Shame to hear about Miss Holden being attacked like that on our city streets. Glad you killed those two scoundrels. Makes you wonder what in God's name this city is coming to."

Longarm said nothing. There was really nothing left to say. Joe Bean had beaten him because when it came to the thousand dollars, he said he'd already spent it on Lizzy's behalf and there was no proof that he was lying.

But they would meet again. Longarm knew it with every fiber of his being, and when they did, the talking would be over and the bullets would be flying.

Chapter 5

When Longarm returned to his rooms, he found Lizzy sitting on his threadbare couch eating an apple and reading the newspaper. She was naked except for one of his old shirts, and she looked up at him with a gorgeous and trusting smile.

Longarm removed his hat and coat. What he had to say next wasn't easy, but there was no way around it, so he blurted, "I didn't get your thousand dollars back, Lizzy."

She laid the newspaper in her lap and kept smiling. "I knew that you wouldn't. Joe Bean isn't the kind of man to give up anything except by force, and you had no evidence against him for an arrest or anything."

"I probably should have forced a fight and ended it right there in that old woman's boardinghouse," Longarm told her as he sat down on the couch. "But the truth is, I promised Mrs. Waite that there would be no trouble in her home and a promise is a promise."

"One I'm glad that you kept. Mrs. Waite is hard on the outside, but inside she's as soft as pudding, and a killing in her boardinghouse would have destroyed her and the business that she completely relies upon in her old age."

"There was one other thing that stopped me from forcing

a fight," Longarm said. "And that is that I once greatly admired Joe Bean and he did save my life down in Taos, New Mexico."

"So you think that you owe him?"

"No," Longarm said, "because I saved him from being lynched one time in Nevada. Joe stepped over the line and a Virginia City lynch mob was ready to hang him high. Joe deserved a rope, but he was my friend and he promised me that he'd never take the law into his own hands again and would become a better man and marshal."

Lizzy took a bite of her apple. "But he didn't."

"No," Longarm said. "And about two years later, a rich mine owner who lived up in Central City was found murdered and the vault he kept in his mansion was emptied. No one knew exactly how much money was in that vault, but it is said to have been thousands, plus loads of expensive jewelry."

"Did Joe Bean kill the mine owner?"

"It couldn't be proved, but the people I worked with thought that he did it for certain. They fired Joe and warned him to stay out of trouble."

"But he didn't."

"Joe is a gambler and not a very good one. When the money he'd stolen ran out, he became a bounty hunter and a hired gun. He had a reputation that scared people nearly to death, so he rarely had to kill anyone. But I've heard dozens of stories about him over the years . . . all of them bad."

Longarm took in a deep breath. "Today Joe Bean told me that he had gold fever and that he knew about your father finding gold up near your Salida ranch. He also implied that he knew that before you hired him. Joe said that's where he expected we'd meet the next time."

Lizzy shook her head and looked down at her hands. When she saw that they were shaking, she clasped them together tightly and looked up at Longarm. "I'm convinced that Mr. Bean thinks I know where the gold is that Father found up near our ranch. When I return to the ranch Joe will trap me, then torture me to death trying to get me to talk."

"*Do* you know where your father found his gold?"

"No, of course not! I had been living in St. Louis and was engaged to be married, remember?"

"I remember," Longarm said. "But Joe probably thinks that your father sent you a letter containing information about where he had his gold strike."

"He didn't."

Longarm considered this for a moment. "But if Joe *thinks* he did, then he'll want to find out for sure and he'll want to do that up by Salida."

"I have to go back to my ranch," Lizzy said. "I can't just stay away out of fear."

Longarm disagreed and told her so. "Lizzy, you told me you sold off all the livestock. Why don't you just sell the ranch and go somewhere else? If you never go to Salida, then Joe will have to figure you don't know where your father's gold is hidden. After a while, he'll give up waiting for you to return, lose interest, and move on to something else."

"That would be the smart thing to do," Lizzy said, looking right at Longarm. "But how would you feel if someone was keeping you from going to the only place where you'd ever been really happy? The place where both your parents are buried as well as your childhood sweetheart? Where all your childhood memories are the only things you have left to make you smile?"

Longarm had to be honest. "I wouldn't stand for that. No one can tell me where I can live . . . or not live."

"I feel exactly the same way," Lizzy replied with steel in her voice.

"But there's another thing you have to consider," said Longarm. "It's possible, maybe more than possible, that Joe was behind your father's death in the first place"

"Which is why I can't go alone," she replied. "Custis, I've been thinking about us all morning."

"That's not a smart thing to do," Longarm said. "I've already told you that I'd make a poor husband or partner. I like what I do and I'm always on the move going from one assignment to the next. I can't be tied down to a person or a place for too long."

"Are you sure of that?"

"Yes," he said without hesitation.

But Lizzy wasn't one to give up easy. "People change, Custis. They change all the time. If you'll give up being a lawman, I'll give you half my ranch and you don't even have to marry me if you don't want to."

Longarm came to his feet. "What the hell are you talking about?"

"I'm talking about *us*!" She stood and put her arms around his neck. "We could make a wonderful life together."

"But I'm no rancher! Not even a cowboy. I don't know anything about . . ."

Lizzy silenced his protests with a kiss. "I know enough about ranching for the both of us and you can learn to be a good rancher and husband. I'd be a wonderful teacher. I'd make it fun for us both."

"No."

Lizzy stepped back and the lightness went out of her voice. "Custis, I'm going up to the ranch and I'm going to use the three thousand dollars I have left to stock it with horses and cattle. It's a very good ranch. Eighteen hundred acres of fine grassland and some tall timber to sell on the side. There's a big stream that runs through the meadow and the ranch house isn't going to impress a rich man, but it's well built and will stand up against time and the weather for longer than we'd both live."

Longarm threw up his hands and then let them fall to his sides. "I just can't, Lizzy."

"If you don't go with me, Joe Bean will show up and

then he'll torture me to death trying to find out where my father found his gold. I'll die in agony while he is laughing. I expect he'll rape me, do things to me that are unspeakable. And when he's broken me and I still can't tell him where to find the gold, then he'll kill me and ride away . . . or else stay and live on my ranch where my parents are buried and where I died screaming."

Longarm looked into her dark eyes, and he knew that what she had just told him was the God's honest truth. Without him at her side, Joe Bean would come and torture Lizzy to death.

The question that Longarm had to face was, could he live knowing that?

"Lizzy," he finally said with a catch in his injured throat, "I . . . I can't let that happen to you."

Hope sprang into her eyes again. "There's only one way to stop it from happening and that's to come with me to the ranch. We can start rebuilding just as soon as the snow melts. Even before. And maybe . . . just maybe . . . you'll change your mind and fall in love with me and we can live happily ever after."

"Maybe."

Lizzy threw back her head and laughed with joy.

"We'll raise lots of kids! Raise horses and cattle and grow old and content together. Does that really sound so terrible, Custis?"

"No. It sounds good. But somehow, we'll still have to put Joe Bean down for good. He won't let us live in peace so long as he thinks there is a fortune in gold to be had."

"We can handle Mr. Bean together. We can always watch each other's back. We can lay a trap, if you think that would work." Lizzy threw herself into his arms. "Custis, if last night meant anything at all, then say yes!"

Longarm took a very deep breath, then he swallowed hard and heard himself whisper the word "Yes."

"Oh, God!" she cried, bouncing up and down on her

bare feet and showering his rugged face with kisses. "We'll be so happy together! You'll never regret doing this. Custis, I swear on my father's grave that I will make it my mission to see that you will never regret a single second of our new life together!"

Longarm kissed her deeply and nodded his head, pretty much convinced that she was right. Swept up by her happiness and his own emotions, he scooped Lizzy up in his arms and carried her into his bedroom, where they made love yet again. Wild, passionate love that bound them together as if they had just sealed their marriage.

"Maybe you just planted a seed in me," she said, tears leaking out of the corners of her dark eyes. "Maybe you just planted our first baby."

Longarm nodded with understanding, and they lay still for a good hour while his mind tried to come to terms with giving up his life as a deputy United States marshal. He'd have to give up these small rooms, which weren't all that special, but he'd called them home for at least the last three years. And there were friends that he'd sorely miss, friends like his boss, Billy Vail. And women. He'd known and loved so many Denver women. But by jingo, he could do it. He had to do it because Lizzy was a dead woman without him at her side.

Things were moving too fast, but dammit, he had a feeling that perhaps he could be a rancher and a husband and a father. Maybe it was worth his best try. Lizzy was a remarkable woman. Beautiful. Brave and smart. Together, they could have fine, handsome sons and lovely daughters, and he did like kids . . . well, at least he liked them okay after they got out of diapers and had some teeth to eat with.

"You'll have to turn in your badge," she was saying as she leaned over Longarm and kissed his chest and stomach. "And I think that I should be with you when that happens this afternoon."

Longarm stiffened. "This afternoon?"

"Why wait, darling?"

He looked up at the ceiling, feeling Lizzy sliding down his body and starting to do things that he thought he didn't want to do again so soon. But his manhood had a mind of its own, and in a few minutes she took him into her mouth. Nodding weakly, Longarm said, "Yeah, we'll go to the office and I'll resign today."

Lizzy laughed and enthusiastically went to work on him and just like magic, all of Longarm's doubts and worries were suddenly gone.

Chapter 6

By the time they reached the Federal Building, Longarm was having second thoughts about giving up his career. It was his life, and although it hadn't been an easy life and he hadn't made much money, he still loved the thrill of the chase and the challenge of matching wits with criminals on the run.

"Lizzy," he said as they stood beside a snowbank and looked at the Federal Building, "I'm beginning to wonder if this is really the right thing to do for us."

"Of course it is!" she said, giving him a hug, kissing his cheek, and then slipping her hand down to seductively rub his crotch. "Everything is going to work out beautifully. You'll love our new ranch and the life you'll be starting with me. But . . . if you really don't want to do this . . ."

Longarm growled, "Oh, hell, Lizzy, I can always come back begging for my badge if you decide you've made a bad bargain and want to kick me out of your ranch house."

"*Our* ranch house," she corrected. "Everything up there is going to belong to us both. We're equal partners."

"That's being pretty generous seeing as how your father and mother founded the ranch and then built it up."

"They'd have loved and approved of you, Custis. I just

know that they would have." As if to verify that fact, Lizzy gazed up at the sky and said, "Hi, Father. Hi, Mother! Aren't I marrying a fine handsome man! One you would have been happy to have called your son."

Longarm shook his head in wonder and took Lizzy's gloved hand. "Come on," he said, dragging her up the steps. "My boss, Marshal Billy Vail, is going to be one unhappy man when I give him my badge. I might as well warn you that he'll try to talk me out of it even with you at my side."

"Let him!" Lizzy laughed. "But Mr. Vail can talk himself blue in the face for all I care because he isn't going to change either of our minds . . . is he?"

"Nope," Longarm said, summoning all the conviction he could muster. "Once I've made up my mind on a thing, I am not one to back out of it."

"I know that," Lizzy said. "And I'm exactly the same way. After you quit your job, we can go find a justice of the peace and get married."

"Whoa!" Longarm stopped halfway up the stairs.

"What's the matter?"

"Well . . . well, I'd sorta like to have a little more time to get used to that marrying thing," he blurted.

"I'm not going to give you half of my ranch if you aren't even willing to give me your name." Lizzy suddenly looked hurt. "Don't you want to marry me, Custis?"

"Well, sure I do, but . . . but I'd just like a little time to get used to the idea. Lizzy, I swore I'd always be a bachelor, and now here you are talking me into giving up my badge, leaving all my friends and my life here in Denver, and getting married. All in the same breath."

She studied his eyes. "Tell you what. Quit your federal officer's job and hand over your badge, then come up to the ranch and spend the rest of the winter with me. If by springtime you're not the happiest man in all of Colorado, then you can ride away and I won't try to stop you. How's that?"

"That seems like a reasonable proposition," Longarm told her, trying to mask the immense relief he was suddenly feeling inside. "I just don't like to be pushed into things, Lizzy. I'm a man kinda set in my ways, and they're ways that took a long time to form and they won't be changed overnight."

"I understand," she said, her expression serious and her tone of voice matter-of-fact. "But I'm completely sure that you'll not only come to love me, but also enjoy the ranching life. You're going to love our ranch and the country up there, Custis. Why, the air is as pure and sweet as the finest French white wine, and it'll make you just as giddy."

"I'd better not be giddy when Joe Bean shows up with his gun."

"Let's not talk or even think about him for a while, Custis. Come on! Let's break the news to your boss and then start packing. Denver is a fine city, but it's still a city and I'm feeling hemmed in and tired of all the people."

"All right," Longarm agreed as they continued on up the stairs and into the large government building.

"You're what!" Billy cried, jumping up from behind his desk.

"I'm quitting and handing over my badge," Longarm said, laying his badge on Billy's large mahogany office desk. "Lizzy . . . I mean Miss Holden . . . and I are getting hitched."

"When? Why!"

"This coming spring," Lizzy told the astonished and upset marshal. "And you will, of course, be invited along with your family. The wedding will be up at our ranch near Salida."

"Your ranch? *What* ranch!"

Longarm frowned. "Billy, there is no call to shout and get upset. Miss Holden owns a cattle ranch up near Salida. That's where we're going and . . . and if everything goes well, we'll be married this spring and I'll become a cattle rancher."

"Bullshit!" Billy bit his tongue and took a deep, steadying breath. "Excuse my profanity, Miss Holden, but this whole thing sounds bizarre."

"Why!" Lizzy snapped, her own voice rising. "You're a married man, I take it."

"Well, yes, I am," Billy stammered, "but what has that got to do with anything?"

"Are you *happily* married, Mr. Vail?"

"Very happily married, but . . ."

"Then why is it so hard for you to let your friend and deputy seek the same kind of marital bliss that you are obviously enjoying?"

"Because I'm Billy Vail and he's Custis Long!" Billy slammed the desk with his closed fist so hard that his coffee cup jumped an inch. "He's Longarm. Custis is the long arm of the law and I'll have you know that he's the most feared federal marshal in the entire West. Miss Holden, Custis isn't just a deputy federal marshal, he's . . . he's a *legend*!"

Longarm blushed with embarrassment, but Lizzy folded her arms across her chest. "A legend with a bull's-eye on his chest! Custis has done his time and put his life on the line for you long enough. I'm offering him not only all my love and my life, but a half interest in one of the sweetest ranches in the whole Rocky Mountains!"

"He'll never be a rancher."

"Billy, I just could be," Longarm said quietly. "I've just never tried that before."

"You'd hate it!" Billy exploded. "Ranchers fix fences. They're out freezing all winter in the snow trying to feed livestock and slogging through the mud messing around

48

with cattle. They have to pull calves from the butt end of their unhappy mothers, for hell sakes!"

Longarm's jaw dropped. "They do?"

"Sure they do!" Billy roared. "And that is the very last thing that you want to do night after cold, miserable night."

"Enough of that talk, Mr. Vail!" Lizzy stormed. "Ranchers do work hard, and I'll admit that sometimes the work is dirty and even tedious. But they also take great pride in building their herds, watching the seasons change on their own land, and going to bed at night in their own house beside their own fireplace. They eat regular meals, and they even have loving families that help them build a dream and a profitable ranch."

Billy threw up his hands and collapsed in his desk chair. "Custis," he said, "are you really sure about what you're doing right now? I can see that Miss Holden is lovely and very persuasive . . . but I thought you were a man who knew who he really was and what he wanted out of his life. And that isn't ranching or raising cattle or kids."

"A man can change," Longarm replied. "Billy, I don't mean to hurt your feelings, but you've been out of the field a long, long time while riding that desk chair. Maybe you've forgotten what it feels like to be standing alone in a strange town and facing down some crazy bastard with a shotgun. Or sleeping on the cold, hard ground night after night and not having enough food or blankets. And have you tasted burned beans in a while or gotten the scoots because of bad meat or water? Billy, I've been shot, stabbed, clubbed, and knifed more times than I care to remember."

"I know you have," Billy admitted. "And you've always taken the worst cases and the most dangerous chances."

Longarm wasn't finished talking. "I'm not young anymore, Billy. My hands are stiffening and so is my back. I can't draw quite as fast as I once did and my aim might be a little off these days."

"Bullshit! I saw you handle a gun less than a month ago

when we all went out and had a shooting contest. You beat everyone in the building without even seeming to try. You're the best man with a gun or rifle I've ever seen, and that hasn't changed in a month, by Gawd!"

"Well, I do have a way with weapons, I'll admit to that much. But my mind is made up."

"Why!" Billy cried. "No offense, Miss Holden, but how long have you known my best deputy?"

"Time doesn't matter," Lizzy answered. "Some people meet and it's love at first sight. Besides, Custis saved my life yesterday."

Billy turned on Longarm with upraised eyebrows. "Custis, were you the one who killed those two men just a block down the street in that snowstorm?"

"Yup. I shot one and left the other to freeze."

Billy's eyes went to Lizzy, who nodded, then they returned to Longarm. "Did you report their deaths to the locals?"

"Not yet. I've been busy."

"Yeah," Billy said cryptically, shooting a glance back at the smiling Lizzy. "I'm sure that you have. But that doesn't change the fact that there were two dead bodies found frozen in the snow and no one has a clue as to why they died."

"I'll stop in at the police station and make out the standard reports," Longarm promised. "But they were just a couple of muggers who got vicious and were unlucky when I heard Lizzy's cries for help. The truth of the matter is that we did Denver a big favor."

"I'm sure that's true; however . . ."

"There's another thing that you need to know," Longarm said, cutting off his former boss.

"I'm listening."

Lizzy said, "Mr. Joe Bean most likely murdered my father for gold. And he's going to come after me in order to find that gold. Custis and I will have to face up to him and end it at the ranch. Mr. Vail, if Custis chooses to stay here in Denver, then I can live with that and I'll abide by his decision. But rest assured that Mr. Bean means to torture and kill me for certain."

"Joe Bean," Billy whispered. "How did he get involved in this?"

"I hired him to find my father's killer," Lizzy said, "not knowing that Mr. Bean was most likely himself the killer. I made a big mistake."

"Yes, you did," Billy told her. "But right now, it's Custis who seems to be making the mistake."

"No, I'm not," Longarm said with conviction. "Billy, my decision is final. I hope we can remain friends and that you'll come to our wedding this spring. We can put you and your family up at our ranch house."

"That's right," said Lizzy.

"I'll want you to be my best man," Longarm said. "I sure hope you'll accept."

"Of course I will!" Billy said, finally looking pleased.

"Thank you," Longarm said formally. "Now I guess we'd better be going. Lizzy and I have to pack and I have to make out that report for the police."

"Do that," Billy said, suddenly feeling old and deflated as he picked up Longarm's badge and studied it with sadness. "If you want to change your mind someday, this badge will always be waiting for you, and there might even be a raise in pay and rank."

"Thanks, Billy. But I doubt that will be happening."

"You never know."

"I know."

Billy stood. "Miss Holden, I wish you and Custis nothing but happiness together. And as for Joe Bean, well, just be very, very careful."

"We mean to."

Billy stuck out his hand, and both Longarm and Lizzy shook it with great formality.

"Good-bye," Longarm said.

"I'll never be able to replace you, Custis."

"You have some good young men coming up in this department."

"Yeah, but none of them will ever be able to carry your water."

"Thanks," Longarm said. "I appreciate the compliment."

When Longarm and Lizzy reached the door, Billy said, "Uh . . . wait just a moment there."

They turned and saw Billy coming around his desk with a shiny double-barreled shotgun. "This was a present to me from the Vice President of the United States after I ran down and killed one of the West's worst murderers, Jade Crenshaw."

"I remember," Longarm said, his mind going back a good many years. "I had just joined the force and you were the hero of the town."

"That was quite some time ago," Billy said modestly. "A lot of water has gone under the bridge since then. But do take the shotgun, Custis. Take it and use it when Joe Bean shows up. Give him both barrels and blow him straight to hell, or else he'll do the same to you and Miss Holden without hesitation or any regrets."

"I will kill Joe Bean, given my first opportunity."

"You'll have that opportunity," Lizzy said. "He'll come looking for us this spring, if not before."

Longarm took the shotgun, and then told Billy how much he appreciated the gift. "I'll take good care of it."

"You do that and it'll take good care of you in return," Billy promised.

There was nothing left to say after that, so Longarm and Lizzy left the office and headed out to the street and a new way of life.

"Nice shotgun," Lizzy said. "Giving it to you was quite an honor."

"I'll miss Billy," Longarm admitted. "I've worked for

him for quite a few years and never had a finer man for a boss."

"Well," Lizzy said, taking his arm, "from now on you'll be your own boss. No more orders. You make the calls."

"We'll make them together," Longarm said. "Remember, I don't know a thing about raising cows."

"It's not that hard to learn and you'll be good at it," she said reassuringly. "And I'm a good teacher."

"I'll just bet you are," Longarm said with a wink and a smile. "But so am I. In fact, when we get back to my rooms, I'm going to teach you a new position that we can do. One that will make you smile for the next twenty-four hours."

It was her turn to blush. "You promise?"

"I promise."

Lizzy burst out laughing and her face flushed with excitement. "I can't wait," she said as she began to pull him along the icy sidewalk faster and faster.

Chapter 7

Longarm and Lizzy left Denver on a stagecoach the following Monday morning. The weather had turned unusually warm, and all the city streets and roads were gutters of pale brown mud. Before leaving, Longarm had dutifully made his report to the local police regarding the two dead muggers, and then he'd said good-bye to the other residents in his building.

There were many tears and heartfelt farewells, and Longarm quickly got to the point where he just wanted to get on with his new life as a cattle rancher. Several of his peers from the Federal Building had come by his rooms, and they'd wanted to give him a big farewell office party, but he'd politely yet firmly declined.

"I really don't like good-byes," he told them, "but I'm honored by the sentiment."

"You'll be back in the spring," one of the deputies boldly predicted. "A man like you will go crazy riding herd on some shitty, snotty cows. There will be snow up to the treetops and you'll have to chop ice with a pick and ax. The nights up there in that country are so cold your bones will ache."

55

"You might be right about deep snow," Longarm agreed, "but I doubt that it's going to be as tough ranching as you are making it out to be."

"I'd bet that you'll hate every damned minute of it," the deputy said, looking smug and confident of his prediction. "You were made to be a lawman, not a cowman."

Lizzy gave the lawman a hard look, and practically shoved him out the door. Then, because Longarm was looking kind of sad, she gave him a special treat after unbuttoning his trousers. But even so, Longarm was subdued and unusually quiet until they at last climbed onto the stagecoach and finally bade Denver farewell.

There were three other passengers heading up into the mountains. A well-dressed and prosperous-looking older couple, both very hard of hearing, and a tall, handsome young cowboy with a black eye, an arm in a sling, and a sad, hangdog expression.

To avoid being overheard by the other passengers, Lizzy leaned over to whisper in Longarm's ear. "You've ridden me so hard and often these last four days that it was all that I could do to climb onto this stagecoach because I'm sore between my legs."

Longarm managed a tolerant smile, and realized that he had been a little overzealous in his lustful lovemaking. "Once I get busy on the ranch, I probably won't have the time or energy to do it so much, Lizzy."

"I hope that's not the case," she replied. "When we get to the ranch, I should warn you that it'll be shut up and cold, but we'll make it nice and cozy in a few hours, and then we'll build a fire and lie naked on a bearskin rug by the hearth. My father shot that old grizzly about ten years ago, and ever since I was a young girl I used to fantasize about making love on that thick bearskin."

"You've got the generous heart of a saint, but the wicked mind of a young whore when it comes to that stuff," Longarm told her. "It's a nice combination and one I intend to exploit."

"Exploit me every chance you get, big boy!"

The injured cowboy gave them a wink. The old couple smiled and said, "Where are you two headed?"

"Up near Salida," Lizzy answered.

"Do you have a ranch up there?"

"We do," Lizzy said proudly. "We have a cattle ranch."

"Hope your cattle haven't frozen to death," the old lady said sweetly. "We live about sixty miles from Salida and it's been a long, hard winter."

"It'll soon be spring," Lizzy said, trying to keep things on a positive note. "And all my cattle were sent to market and sale."

"Probably wise to sell 'em off," the old woman said. "Spring is still three months away in that country . . . if you're lucky. There's snow up at our ranch right to the rafters and icicles longer than pine trees. Up where we live, it's been colder than a witch's caress."

"She's right," her husband added. "I brought my yard cows into the barn just before Christmas, but instead of milk, they gave me icicles!"

They both laughed at the joke, the old man slapping his knee and howling.

"You folks don't know what cold is really like," the young cowboy finally opined. "I grew up in northern Montana where the winters make Colorado winters look like a Mexican heat wave. Why, it's colder up in Montana than a mother-in-law's kiss. Once they brought us a polar bear down from the Klondike, but the poor critter started shiverin' like a lizard lookin' for a hot rock, and then he froze solid as bone . . . and that was in July!"

Longarm crossed his arms across his chest and said, "You people sure like to tell some big old windies. I've been up in the Rockies in winter and it wasn't *that* bad."

"How long has it been since you've wintered up in real high country?" the old woman asked.

"A while," Longarm admitted. He looked at the cowboy. "Are you going to a ranch to mend?"

"There's no time for a cowboy to mend, mister. I'm going to find work because I couldn't find anything in Denver. But heck, there's too many folks there anyways. I don't do well in cities, and I can still get more hard ranch work done with one arm than your run-of-the-mill cowboy can do with both arms."

"Are you really good with cattle and horses?" Lizzy asked the young man.

"Good? Why, ma'am, I was born to cowboy! I grew up ropin' and ridin' broncs when I was knee-high to a jackrabbit. I can rope a mosquito on the fly and, if I'm in a hurry to get somewhere, I'll saddle up and ride a Texas tornado."

"If you're so good, how'd you break that arm?" Longarm asked.

"It was broken in a barroom fight over a woman," the young man sadly confessed. "I didn't know she had a jealous husband sitting right behind me playing billiards. He broke his cue over my arm."

"So he broke your arm just for talking to his wife?" Lizzy asked.

The cowboy blushed. "Actually, I was doing a lot more than talkin' to her, ma'am. That's why I guess I deserved havin' my arm broke. Better'n getting my neck broke or my noggin split wide open with that cue, which he was intent on doin' until I beaned him with an eight ball right between the eyes. Even then, I was in a bad situation because he had a lot of friends in that saloon."

"So that means that you had to make a real fast exit, I suspect," Longarm said.

"I did. Right through an open window. Landed in the alley on a pile of frozen dog crap and some tin cans that cut me up a little. But I got off good, I guess, considerin' my foolishness."

"Women can make a man foolish," Longarm said, getting a dig in the ribs from Lizzy.

"What's your name, cowboy?"

"Jesse Horn. My uncle was Tom Horn. I expect you might have heard of him."

"I have," Longarm said. "Matter of fact, we met one time down in Prescott, Arizona. Your uncle could speak Apache, and I was told he helped to talk Geronimo into surrendering to General Miles Nelson down in a place in Old Mexico called Skeleton Canyon."

"Yes, sir, he sure enough did that!" Jesse said proudly. "Tom taught me how to track, hunt, shoot, and fight. He'd tell you he taught me all there is to know about women, but I have learned he was deficient in that respect. Truth is, I don't understand a thing about 'em."

"Neither do I," Longarm said with a smile. He was beginning to think that he liked this young cowboy with the broken arm.

Lizzy asked, "Jesse, have you ever worked up around Salida?"

"No, ma'am. But high country is high country and a cow acts just as contrary in New Mexico or Arizona as it does in Colorado or Montana. I like cows, but the truth is that next to pretty women, I mostly love fast horses."

Lizzy nodded and said, "I sold all my cattle, but still have a lot of mustangs on the ranch and up in the hills that are running wild. Jesse, would you be interested in helping Custis and me catch some of them?"

The tall cowboy's eyes lit up. "Why, sure I would! But do you mean in the snow?"

"That's right," Lizzy said. "That's the best time to track and lasso them. Do you think you could ride and rope mustangs in heavy timber with snow lying deep on a mountainside?"

The cowboy flexed the fingers of his right hand to prove that his right arm wasn't going to interfere with his hands. "I can rope anything that moves, ma'am."

Lizzy looked at Longarm. "What do you think? We're going to need some help. I just didn't plan on hiring anyone for another month or two, but Jesse here might just work out for us."

"Sure I would! I'll work for beans, warm blankets, and fifty cents a day until I get full use of my arm back," the cowboy told them. "I can chop wood and haul water as good with one arm as with two. I ain't a slacker and I'll stay sober as long as I'm on the ranch. And I'll even let you warn the women up in Salida that I'm not at all to be trusted."

"Sounds like we've just hired a man," Longarm said. "But don't you think that I ought to tell him about Joe Bean?"

Lizzy nodded. "Go ahead. It's only fair that he know the trouble we have before he hires on."

"Who's Joe Bean?" Jesse asked.

"I'm surprised that you've never heard of him," Longarm told the cowboy. "Joe Bean was once a deputy United States marshal. He taught me how to track men and to keep from getting killed. He's tough, smart, and brave."

"But now he's your enemy?"

"Yes," Lizzy said. "I'm pretty sure that he killed my father, and I know he thinks gold is to be found on our ranch, or very close to it. He also feels certain that I know where that gold is to be found."

"Do you?" Jesse asked.

"No," Lizzy replied. "I don't know anything about any gold. But my father was always looking for it even though he was a successful and respected cattle rancher. I can't tell you all the times that Father went searching for gold instead of strays."

"Did you ever see *any* gold he found, ma'am?"

"As a matter of fact I did," Lizzy said. "But only an occasional nugget. A few were large and worth quite a bit of money. Father always found enough to feed his gold fever, and he never gave up the idea that he would someday be a rich man . . . not from the ranch and our cattle herd . . . but from a gold mine he'd one day discover."

"So this Joe Bean thinks you know where there is gold and he wants to force you into telling him?"

"That's about the size of it," Longarm said. "Joe Bean will lie in wait and try to get the drop on me or Lizzy. Once he has either of us alone and lined up in his rifle sights, he'll mostly like try to wing us and take us hostage. If he succeeds, he can force Lizzy to tell him where the gold is hidden."

Jesse looked confused. "But the lady just said that she doesn't know where there is gold to be found."

"True," Longarm said. "But he's the kind of man who would just think that the more you said one thing, the more likely it was that the other was true."

"This Joe Bean sounds like a mighty tough hombre and I am beginning to understand," Jesse said, smile fading.

"I hope that you do," Lizzy told him. "Because Joe Bean is a very dangerous and cunning man. If you go to work for me, he might even decide to kill or capture and try to beat information out of you."

"That's right," Longarm said. "And we don't want you to get hurt or killed on our account."

Jesse's jaw muscles tightened. "You just tell me what this Bean fella looks like, and after that I can take care of things on my own. Women I fear, but not men. I'm as good a shot with a gun or rifle as Uncle Tom, and he was about the best anyone ever seen along the southern border. He killed more Apache and Mexicans than Buffalo Bill killed buffalo, or so he told everybody. But Uncle Tom liked to stretch the truth a mite."

Longarm and Lizzy exchanged glances, and then Lizzy said, "Jesse Horn, if you're willing to work for beans, a bed, and fifty cents a day to start, you're hired."

"I do and I appreciate the job," Jesse told them with a grin. "Do you have a bunkhouse with a good potbelly stove?"

"No," Lizzy said. "But we have an extra bedroom off the kitchen. You'll be near the stove and plenty warm until the weather turns nice."

"Sounds good," Jesse said with a winning smile. "I'm much obliged. There are plenty of good cowboys out of work this bad time of the year. Some of them ride the grub line and do odd chores for a meal or two, but that's mean livin'. I was prepared for it, but hopin' I might get lucky and land a steady job. Looks like I just did."

The old rancher, who had been silent and listening to the conversation, cleared his throat. "Young fella, if it don't work out with them two, you can look us up and we'll put you on the payroll. We have a ranch near Buena Vista."

Jesse Horn beamed and let out a laugh. "Well, ain't that just something! I got *two* job offers with a broken arm while dead broke ridin' a stagecoach. My, oh, my! If I ever get into a fix again, I'll remember where to go lookin' for work instead of ridin' all over the countryside beggin' for beans and a warm winter bed."

Longarm chuckled. He figured that Jesse would be a darned good hand and a capable man to have while he learned the cattle-ranching business. It also helped that Jesse was apparently good with a gun, but Longarm hoped that the young cowboy would never have to face Joe Bean. He might be fast and straight-shootin', but Longarm doubted the young cowboy had ever faced the likes of Joe

Bean. Facing Bean was a whole lot more dangerous than facing the average man whose wife's virtue might be on the verge of being compromised by the young Montana cowboy.

Chapter 8

Their stagecoach limped into Buena Vista with two broken spokes on the rear wheel. The wheel wobbled so badly that it seemed a miracle that they had even gotten that far.

"We're gonna have to lie over until we get that wheel fixed," the driver said as he stopped before the town's only blacksmith shop. "But we'll be leaving first thing in the morning."

"Driver, it's only noon," Lizzy protested as the old couple's baggage was being unloaded. "Surely, you can just replace the wheel and let us be on our way to Salida."

"Sorry, ma'am. Company says that we always fix the wheels, not buy new ones. They operate on a real tight budget."

"I never heard of such a thing!" Lizzy groused.

"The three of you would be welcome to stay at our ranch," the old rancher said, "but it's out quite a ways."

"There's a nice hotel just up the street," the driver said. "I'm sure that you can all get rooms there and we'll get a fresh and early start tomorrow morning. Salida is only about twenty-five miles, so we should be there by early afternoon, if we don't have any more problems."

"And by that you mean broken wheels?" Longarm asked.

"Wheels, axles, or horses," the driver said as he climbed down off his seat. "They can all cause you problems and delays. On top of that, we've had three holdups in the last two months."

Longarm was instantly alert. "In this area?"

"That's right. I was drivin' when one of 'em happened three weeks ago. Five masked riders shot the wheel horse and when it went down, the stagecoach almost flipped over on a steep and narrow downhill grade. It was all that I could do to get the team under control and to keep the stagecoach from going over the edge into a deep gorge. Next thing I knew, the masked robbers were galloping up and demanding that all the passengers get out of the coach and hand over all their jewelry and money."

"Were you carrying any gold or bank currency?" Longarm asked.

"No, sir. But a couple of passengers were pretty well heeled in terms of cash in their wallets. And one of their wives wore a diamond big enough to choke a coyote. So by the time they emptied our pockets and took the jewelry, I'd guess they got away with a couple of thousand dollars."

"And no one tried to resist?" Jesse asked with amazement.

"Nope," the driver said. "The passengers were older folks, and I reckon they were wise not to put up a fight and get killed. Me, I don't get paid to put up a fight either."

"Well," Jesse said, "if they try to rob this stagecoach, they're gonna find things are a whole lot more troublesome."

The cowboy looked at Longarm and Lizzy, who both nodded in agreement. Longarm said, "Driver, when you get close to where you were held up the last time, shout a warning so we can be ready."

"I will," the driver said, "but if bullets start flying, I'm diving off this coach and running for cover. Up in the box, you're a big target."

Lizzy nodded, not seeing that there was any choice in the matter.

They said good-bye to the older couple, who had a buckboard and one of their cowboys waiting. "Good luck in Salida," the older woman said. "Hope that you find some gold up there."

"I doubt that we will," Lizzy said as they trudged up the street with Longarm and Jesse carrying her luggage.

The Buena Vista Hotel was one of the nicest establishments in that part of the country. Having burned down twice, it had been rebuilt the third time with bricks and was three stories tall. The lobby was elegant and large, the restaurant renowned for its cuisine. There was a nice saloon off to one side, and so after Lizzy paid for their rooms, they went down to the restaurant for a meal and a beer.

Afterward, Jesse came up to Longarm and said, "I appreciate the room that Miss Lizzy rented for me. I ain't used to such nice accommodations. But I'm flat broke and I was wondering if I could borrow a little money against my first month's pay."

"How much do you need?"

"Well," Jesse said, "I sure need some new socks and underwear. My boots are near worn out, but they can wait another month. I could use a pair of heavy woolen gloves 'cause I know it'll be cold working outdoors for the next month or two. And I wouldn't mind a couple dollars so that I could buy supper and a few drinks before I pack it in tonight."

"How about I loan you ten dollars?" Longarm said, knowing the cowboy was good for the money. "Would that do you?"

"It'd do me fine," Jesse said with a grateful smile. "And I'll work it off right away."

"At fifty cents a day it'll take you nearly the whole first

month," Longarm warned, giving the young cowboy ten dollars.

"I always pay off my debts," Jesse said.

"Good to hear that," Longarm said, heading out the door.

When he got back to the room he'd share with Lizzy, he kicked off his boots and tossed his coat and hat on a chair. The room was spacious and clean, the bed nice and soft.

"This isn't too tough to take," Longarm said. "I was getting a little tired of sitting in that stagecoach hour after hour."

"Me, too," Lizzy said. "Actually, it's probably a good thing we stopped for the night. When we get to our ranch, there will be plenty to do before we can get to bed tomorrow night."

"I expect so," Longarm said, lying on the bed and closing his eyes. "But to tell you the truth, riding in a jouncing stagecoach hour after hour just takes the spunk out of me. And the dust! Why, you either gotta pull the curtains shut and sit in the dark, or you open the curtains and eat dust until your gullet feels like sand."

Lizzy undressed and lay down beside him. "We haven't done anything together since Denver." She gave his limp rod a playful tug. "You up to messin' around some, Custis?"

"I am," he said, rolling over and kissing her lips. "Nothing better than a little afternoon lovemaking."

Lizzy nodded in eager agreement and a few minutes later, she was riding Longarm with a flushed look of joy on her pretty face. Longarm was also grinning widely, and when he was near to getting ready to explode, he rolled Lizzy off, mounted her, and drove his manhood in and out of her until she was clawing at his back and howling like a wildcat.

Longarm and Lizzy climaxed at the same moment and temporarily lost their senses in the crashing waves of passion. Spent at last, they collapsed beside each other and fell into a deep and refreshing sleep.

Meanwhile, Jesse was finishing up his shopping and thinking that he would have a few beers in the saloon and maybe even get into a poker game for a few hands to see if he could get lucky. It would be fine to be able to win enough money to pay Longarm back so that he'd not be working off his debt for the rest of this month while chasing cows and chopping wood for the stove.

The beer was cold and delicious, and Jesse still had two dollars when he sat down with three men to play a few games of cards. One of the men had the appearance of being a professional gambler, and he had a pretty young woman hanging over his shoulder.

Jesse winked at the young woman, and she couldn't help but smile. He figured that the gambler had more money than *he* did, but the guy was homely as a mud fence. Jesse played a few hands without managing to lose more than seventy-five cents. The young woman kept watching him, and Jesse found that he was having trouble keeping his mind on the game.

"Guess I'll quit," Jesse said after he lost another two bits. "I can see that luck isn't with me today."

The gambler, a thin-faced man with a weak chin, just looked at Jesse and said, "You lost one dollar, but you still have another. Might be that your luck could change if you wasn't so chicken as to quit."

Jesse's face flushed with anger. "No man calls me chicken," he warned. "Maybe I just don't like your company."

The gambler laughed and it wasn't a nice sound. "Cowboy," he said, "I knew from the minute you sat down at this table that you were a quitter and a cheapskate. Knew that you didn't have any *real* money and that you were too dumb to be a good player."

Jesse's fist shot across the table and latched onto the gambler's throat. Even with one hand, he was still the better man, and he lifted the gambler right out of his chair and then hurled him into the back wall. When the gambler's eyes stopped rolling around in his homely face like black beans in a canning jar, the man foolishly tried to tear a derringer out from under his dirty silk vest. Jesse took offense to that move, and kicked the man under the chin so hard that his head snapped back and he lost consciousness.

"Fair fight, wasn't it?" he asked the pretty girl.

"It was fair all right, but you didn't have to kick Clyde like that. You might have broke his neck and killed him!"

Jesse realized this might be true. Worried, he bent over the unconscious gambler and checked his pulse. It was still beating, so Jesse grinned and said, "He's just out for a while. Maybe he learned some manners."

"I doubt it."

"You his girl?"

"He brought me to Buena Vista when I fell on some hard times. I was stayin' with him looking for something better."

"You just found something better," Jesse promised, taking the girl by the arm and asking, "What's your name?"

"Teresa. Teresa O'Connell."

"Well, Teresa, I'm Jesse and I have a nice room upstairs. How about coming up to visit with me for a while?"

"You got any money besides what you left the table with?"

Jesse bent back over and emptied the gambler's wallet. "Must be twenty or twenty-five dollars here. That enough for you, honey?"

"Sure is!" she said, slipping her arm into his.

"Let's go." Jesse looked at the three other poker players. "You can divide up Clyde's chips and tell him when he awakens that I took his woman and a few dollars to keep us both happy."

"He'll come to kill you for what you done," one of the players warned.

"Tell him that I'm in room number four upstairs and that I'll expect him to knock before I open the door. After that, I might see how good he flies out the window. He's skinny, maybe he'll sail like an arrow."

Everyone laughed except one player, who said, "Clyde ain't one to let an insult go without payin' a fella back in spades. If I were you, young fella, I'd watch my backside real close. Clyde is a damn good shot."

"So am I," Jesse told the man. "I'm Tom Horn's nephew. You ever heard of Tom Horn?"

"Why, sure I have! He's most as famous as Wild Bill Hickok."

"Well," Jesse said proudly, "I'm a better shot than either one of 'em and you can tell that to Clyde when he wakes up."

With that, Jesse went to the bar, bought a bottle of the keeper's best whiskey, and took the pretty girl upstairs.

"You want to talk a little first?" the girl asked, starting to undress.

"Naw," Jesse said. "Let's just get to it."

"All right," she said sweetly. "But now that I'm your woman, you've got to look after me."

"I do?"

"Sure! Clyde was lookin' after me when you choked and then kicked the shit out of him downstairs. Now you got to do the same as he did."

Jesse shucked out of his pants and shirt and watched as Teresa undressed with more than a little bit of flair. When she was fully naked, Jesse's manhood stood up in appreciation. "Why, Teresa, darlin', you're even prettier without clothes than with 'em . . . and that's rare for most women."

"Thank you," she said, blushing.

Jesse took the girl into his one good arm and pushed her up against the wall. "Spread your pretty legs."

71

Her eyebrows lifted in question. "Jesse, are you really gonna do me standing straight up?"

"Yeah," he said, "for starters."

She swallowed hard. "I never did it that way before."

"Well," Jesse said, jamming his throbbing manhood into her sweet honey pot, "then it's time you learned how good it can feel."

Jesse banged Teresa silly against the wall and rattled the pictures on their hooks. When he finally erupted, the wall lamp crashed to the floor and Teresa fainted.

He carried her to the bed and uncorked the whiskey, then drank it straight from the bottle. "Lordy, oh, lordy," he whispered, looking at her lovely body, "I should have started taking the stagecoach more often. Everything is starting to go my way again."

Teresa soon awakened and eagerly shared his bottle. She kissed his face and said, "I sorta liked it being pinned to the wall like that . . . but I'd like to do it on this bed the next time."

"That's coming up pretty quick, Teresa," he promised. "Now why don't you tell me all about your sweet little self."

"I'm from Iowa," she said. "I'm a farmer's daughter who spent most of my childhood feeding hogs, both the two- and four-legged kind."

Jesse laughed. "You got a nice, funny way with words, girl!"

"And you got a nice way with that big thing that hangs between your legs," she replied. "Are we staying here long?"

"Nope."

"Then where are we going next?"

Jesse hesitated. He wasn't at all sure that Miss Lizzy and Longarm would allow Teresa to go to the ranch, but saw no point in telling this girl about a possible problem.

"We're going to a cattle ranch where we'll work for some very nice folks."

"A cattle ranch!" Teresa sat up in bed. "Jesse, I already done left a pig ranch. Can't see that one with cattle is going to be much better."

"Oh, sure it will be. Cows are a lot more interesting than pigs and they don't smell nearly so bad."

"Cows are dumber than fence posts! At least pigs are smart."

"Give it a try," Jesse told her. "If you don't like it, we'll leave."

"I always wanted to go to California and see the Pacific Ocean," Teresa said. "See San Francisco."

"Might be we'll do that after the spring roundup and branding."

"I hope so," Teresa said. "Clyde said he'd take me to California. We were trying to get up the money to go when you walked into that saloon."

"Sorry to mess up your plans," Jesse said, trying to sound sincere. "But life doesn't always go the way we expect or want it to go."

"You can say that again," Teresa said, pouting.

Jesse pulled the young woman into his arms. "Tonight, I'm going to make you forget all about California."

"You're pretty sure of yourself, aren't you."

"Yep."

She giggled and kissed his lips. "I like you better'n Clyde even if you don't get me to California as fast."

"That's good to hear," Jesse told her as he began to stroke the inside of her silky smooth thighs.

Chapter 9

Jesse Horn awoke in the small hours of the morning to the sound of someone deftly prying open the lock on his hotel room door. He was groggy from too much lovemaking and too much whiskey, so his reaction time was far slower than normal. Even so, he sat up in the semidarkness and scrubbed his eye sockets, and then quickly realized that the intruder could only be Teresa's ex-boyfriend and publicly humiliated gambler, ferret-faced Clyde.

Jesse's six-gun was hanging on a wooden desk chair not quite within his grasp. As the door pushed open, Jesse saw Clyde in the open doorway. The hall lamps revealed a man who was almost too drunk to stand and consumed with rage. And in the few instants that Jesse had left, he saw that the drunken and enraged gambler was holding two pistols out in front of him.

"Teresa!" Jesse shouted, grabbing the sleeping woman and trying to drag her off the bed and onto the floor where she would be at least partially hidden behind cover.

"Teresa O'Connell, you fickle hog-fucked whore!" Clyde shouted, opening fire into the dimly lit room.

Teresa cried out as a bullet struck her somewhere in the back just moments before Jesse could drag her off the bed.

Another bullet creased her skull, and a third tore a gaping wound in her firm buttocks. When she finally hit the floor, she was unconscious and bleeding profusely.

Jesse grabbed his pistol and holster, then threw himself on top of Teresa as Clyde finished emptying one pistol, dropped it, and started marching into the room firing the second weapon.

Fumbling in the darkness, Jesse tore his gun from its holster and raised his well-oiled Colt over the top of the bed just as Clyde tripped over a throw rug, righted himself, and pulled the trigger.

Jesse and Clyde both fired at the same instant. Clyde's slug tore a deep crease across Jesse's cheek and then buried itself into the wall. Jesse's bullet smashed into Clyde's shoulder and spun him halfway around. Jesse fired again and sent the enraged gambler staggering back out into the hallway. Clyde bounced off a wall, leaving a blotch of blood; then he screamed and tried to escape to the stairway that led down to the elegant hallway below.

Naked and filled with the lust for blood and vengeance, Jesse jumped off Teresa's inert body and went charging out the door. He saw Clyde nearing the stairway, and in the hallway's lamplight he had a clear view of his helpless target. Coolly taking aim, he shot Clyde twice in the back, both bullets drilling the man's left scapula and ripping through the drunken gambler's already dying heart. Clyde pitched forward and tumbled end over end down the stairs, landing in the lobby with his pumping blood all over the beautiful carpet.

Jesse marched over to the head of the stairs and gazed down at the dead man with a mixture of fury and satisfaction. "You killed her, you ugly, rotten bastard!" he shouted, taking aim and emptying two more bullets into the gambler's carcass.

Emerging naked from his own room, Longarm grabbed

Jesse's now empty gun and tore it from the cowboy's grip. "Are you crazy!"

"No," Jesse said, slapping a hand against his cheek, which was pouring blood down the side of his face. "That sonofabitch broke into my room and opened fire on me and Teresa."

"Who's Teresa!"

"A girl I found and helped." An unwanted sob escaped the cowboy's lips. "He shot her up, Custis. Maybe killed her for all I know. I should have pushed a dresser up behind the door and kept my gun closer. She warned me that he'd get drunk and go crazy with jealousy!"

Longarm didn't need to hear any more as he raced up the hallway and barged into Jesse's room. The room was dim, but it smelled like a slaughterhouse. "Dammit," Longarm shouted, "where the hell is she!"

"Behind the bed."

"Light a lamp!" Longarm yelled, hurrying over to the young woman bleeding all over the floor behind the bed. "Then go find a doctor!"

When the light went on, Longarm swore in helpless anger when he saw that the woman had been shot three times from behind. He lifted her onto the bed just as Lizzy burst into the room.

"My God, what happened!" Lizzy screamed, hugging a nightgown around her body and staring at the unconscious woman covered with blood.

"Long story, bad ending," Longarm snapped, grabbing a sheet and ripping it into bandaging. "Help Jesse find a doctor and get him up here as fast as you can."

Lizzy took a faltering step toward the bleeding woman. "Who on earth is she?"

"Name's Teresa," Longarm said. "Go get a doctor!"

Lizzy turned and fled the room.

Longarm had suffered many wounds and inflicted even

more. He had learned about bullet wounds the hard way, and now he could see that Teresa's scalp was drenched in blood, but that she was alive and faintly moaning. Longarm slid a finger along her skull, and almost sagged with relief when he determined that the bullet had not entered the brain cavity, but instead only creased bone over her ear. He wrapped her head in a clumsy bandage as tightly as he could to stem the bleeding, and then examined the wound in her back. The gambler's bullet had obviously struck a rib and ricocheted somewhere into the young woman's body. If it had pierced a vital organ, Longarm knew that Teresa was certainly going to die. There was nothing he could do about this wound. It could only be attended to by a surgeon or a very good doctor, so Longarm turned his attention to the woman's serious buttocks injury.

"Nice," he said, muttering to himself as he gently probed the bullet hole and realized that the slug had passed through flesh and muscle and then most likely had exited into the mattress. This wound was bleeding heavily and Longarm wasn't sure how to bandage a woman's butt, so he gently pushed a little of the sheet into the hole and held it tightly in order to lessen the blood loss.

It seemed to take forever before Lizzy, a still naked Jesse, and a very disheveled-looking young doctor arrived.

"How is she?" the doctor asked, hurrying across the room. "Bring that lamp over here so that I have better light!"

"The head wound is just a crease and the bullet passed through her butt. It's the one bleeding the most, but I don't think it's all that serious."

"And what about the one that I can see she took in the rib cage area?"

Longarm shook his head. "I don't know about that one, Doc. Looks to me like it shattered a rib, then caromed off somewhere into her body."

The doctor nodded grimly and his fingers slipped gently into the bullet hole. "This is the one that is probably going to kill her, if I can't get it quickly located and extracted." He took her pulse and said, "I'll need to operate right here and right now and I'll need plenty of assistance."

Longarm started to volunteer, but Lizzy beat him to it and said, "I'll help you. I've some experience."

"Get me some boiling water. Lots of it, and some real bandages or at least plenty of clean laundered hotel towels."

"I'll go downstairs and boil water in the kitchen," Lizzy said. "And I'll bring all the towels you need."

"I'll help you," Jesse said, looking pale and shaken. "Doc, what do you . . ."

"Dammit, cowboy, get dressed and get out of here!" the doctor shouted. "Help that lady get the towels up here to me!"

"What can I do?" Longarm said after Jesse and Lizzy had bolted.

"You can also get dressed and stick around in case I need you to run errands for anything else I may need. I have my surgical instruments in my medical bag. But I have to have a bottle of chloroform as fast as you can get it from my office."

"Where is that?"

The doctor gave Longarm the key to his office and instructions on how to find the place. He also added a few things to the list of emergency medical supplies he needed.

Longarm ran back to his room, pulled on his pants and boots, then went racing out of the hotel to find the chloroform and a few instruments that the doctor had asked him to bring back as soon as possible.

When he had left, the badly shot-up young woman was turning gray, and Longarm thought that her chances of survival were slim. She appeared to have bled gallons and was going into shock. In Longarm's experience, that always meant that death was standing right on the victim's doorstep.

It was eight o'clock and with the good morning light, anyone could see that Jesse's hotel room looked like a slaughterhouse because there was so much spilled blood. Clyde's bullet-riddled body had been removed from the lobby, and the management had immediately set about cleaning the blood-soaked lobby carpet. The manager of the Buena Vista Hotel was furious, and he'd managed to keep the morbid town gawkers from flocking into his hotel.

"I think she's going to live," the doctor finally said, wiping his face and closing up his medical bag. "She's lost a tremendous amount of blood, but I was able to find and extract the slug that entered her back. I don't think it hit any of her vital organs."

Jesse sagged with relief and wrung his calloused hands. Lizzy muffled a low sob, and Longarm just expelled a deep breath.

"What really happened here?" the doctor asked, turning away from his patient and studying all three of them.

Jesse told them exactly what had happened after Clyde had broken into his hotel room with two guns blazing.

When the account was finished, the doctor said, "I understand that the gambler's body was riddled with bullets, some of them entering him after he hit the lobby floor."

"Doc, I'll be the first to admit that I lost my senses for a moment," Jesse told him. "I just went crazy and kept pulling the trigger until my gun was empty."

The doctor studied the young cowboy with deep concern. "You know," he said, "you should have been prepared for what happened. And you should have done a better job protecting this young woman from harm."

"I fully realize that fact," Jesse said, voice heavy with guilt. "There is no doubt that this is all my fault."

"Hardly," the doctor told him, "because the drunken

gambler was bent on murder. But all the same, I think that we got lucky and that this young lady will survive . . . if she gets plenty of bed rest and care. When she comes around, she's going to be weak as a kitten from blood loss."

"I'll see to her care for as long as it takes," Lizzy promised the doctor.

"She can't travel for at least a week. Do you understand?" Lizzy and Longarm nodded.

"I'll have to attend to her every few hours at first and change the bandages frequently. She's still in a lot of danger. Someone will have to stay by her side day and night until I determine that she's out of trouble."

Jesse, Longarm, and Lizzy exchanged glances. "I'm the one that got her into all this trouble," Jesse said. "I'll stay here with her day and night for however long it takes."

"No," Lizzy said. "I'm a woman and better at this sort of thing than you would be."

"But . . ."

Lizzy went to Jesse and touched his ruined face. "You'll need a lot of stitching to close that up, and you'll have a bad scar across that cheekbone for the rest of your life."

"One that I'll sure enough deserve," Jesse said. "I don't care about that, ma'am."

As the doctor left, Longarm stood back from the conversation, deeply troubled by what had happened in this blood-soaked hotel room. To his way of thinking, Jesse should not have gotten the gambler's woman into his bed and into trouble. If the handsome young cowboy had come up to his room after a few beers and simply gone to bed, none of this would have occurred. And then there was the matter of how Jesse had emptied his gun into the dead gambler's body lying at the foot of the stairs. Only a man insane with rage would have committed such a despicable act. Longarm had gunned down a lot of men, but never had he done such a thing as Jesse had done to the gambler no matter how well deserved.

Longarm decided that Jesse Horn would bear very close watching. That he was brave and dangerous was now clearly obvious. Horn's gun had spoken six times, and already the coroner had gotten word out that the gambler had been hit six times.

Longarm knew that was damn good shooting while being shot at. He had to admit that he was impressed with the cowboy's gun skills, but now he was also wary of the young man.

"We can all stay here in Buena Vista," Longarm suggested. "Until this woman has turned the corner."

"No," Lizzy told him. "The ranch is only a day's journey from here. I want you and Jesse to go there and open it up. Get things in order so that when I bring this young woman to the ranch, she'll find it warm and comfortable."

"You're bringing Teresa to your ranch?" Jesse asked.

For a moment, Lizzy's eyes blazed with anger. "What do you expect me to do? Leave her here penniless and helpless among strangers?"

Jesse was embarrassed. "Well, no, but . . ."

"We'll take care of Miss O'Connell until she is back on her feet and well mended," Lizzy vowed. "To do otherwise would be unspeakably heartless and uncharitable. After she's strong enough to stand on her own, she can do what she wants with her life. Hopefully, she's going to have learned a hard lesson about the kind of men she takes up with."

Jesse flushed with shame. "You're talking about *me*, aren't you, Miss Lizzy."

"Yes," she said, giving him a hard stare, "I sure as hell am. When you took this young woman up to this room after humiliating her ex-lover, you should have been prepared to protect her from a deadly retaliation."

"I tried."

"Well," Lizzy said, looking at the unconscious woman, "it would seem that you did a damn poor job of it!"

82

"You're right," Jesse said, hanging his head. "I got her into this and there's no one else to blame but myself."

"I'm glad that you see that plainly," Lizzy shot back, anger still high in her cheeks. "By the looks of this girl, she can't be more than about eighteen or nineteen years old. Do you know anything or even care a little about her?"

"Teresa O'Connell was raised on a hog farm in Iowa," Jesse said. "And she wants me to take her to California someday and I promised that I would."

"And you should!"

"But not for a while," Jesse said.

Lizzy sighed and let her anger slip away. "No," she said. "Not for quite a while . . . if ever."

Longarm had never seen a young man so grieved as Jesse Horn. He looked as if the world had landed right on top of his broad shoulders. And the blood from his facial wound was thick and black on his neck and shirt.

"Come on," Longarm said to the guilt-ridden young cowboy. "The stagecoach is waiting for us. When the driver learned about the shooting, he said he'd hold over until nine o'clock and then he'd have to roll with or without us on board. And you need to get that wound stitched up."

Jesse went over to the bed. He knelt and kissed the unconscious woman on the cheek and whispered something in her ear. When he turned toward Longarm and the door, tears were streaming down his cheeks.

"Custis?"

As Jesse left, Longarm turned back to the room to see Lizzy approaching him. "Custis, here is two hundred dollars. I may be here taking care of this girl longer than a week. You'll need this money to buy supplies in Salida and some horses and other things when you get to the ranch."

"What other things?" Longarm asked.

"Jesse will know what is needed to start getting the

ranch back in operation," Lizzy explained. "I'll trust him to do that right at least."

"He feels real bad already about what happened here last night," Longarm said. "I don't know if we need to ride him too hard for a while."

But Lizzy was of a different frame of mind. "Young Mr. Jesse Horn has a lot to learn, and I'm going to really give him a piece of my mind when I get back to the ranch. And if this girl doesn't survive, I might shoot Jesse dead and drag his body out onto the range for the buzzards and varmints to feed on for the rest of this winter."

"If you plan to shoot him," Longarm suggested, "I'd recommend you tell me first so that I can get the drop on him. Whatever Jesse is, he's awful damned good with a six-gun."

"Yes, I could see that when I looked at the gambler's body down at the foot of the stairs."

"We could use a good man that can also handle a gun," Longarm told her. "Joe Bean might bring a few bad friends."

"I know. I've thought of that."

"Jesse would stand with us in a fight."

"I know that, too," Lizzy agreed. "But after what happened last night, do you think we can trust him?"

Longarm didn't understand. "What do you mean?"

"I mean look what he's done and we've only known him for a day! Custis, the kid is hell on wheels, and who knows what he might do if he somehow decided to turn against us!"

"He won't do that," Longarm said, quite sure he was right.

"Can you really be so certain?"

Longarm considered the question carefully before he answered. "Jesse Horn is a hothead and a wild card. But I think what happened last night in this room has probably changed him for the better. Made him realize the consequences of bad actions."

"You're giving him a lot of credit he may not deserve."

"I'll be watching him every minute," Longarm promised. "If he's really bad, then I'll figure that out soon enough and we'll send him packing."

"And if Jesse decides that he doesn't want to go 'packing,' or maybe even comes to the conclusion that there is gold to be found and that he would be wise to hook up with Joe Bean?"

"Then we've fed the wolf and we're gonna pay dearly for it," Longarm admitted.

"Maybe we should fire him right now. Just tell him to leave."

"He wouldn't."

Lizzy studied Longarm. "What does that mean?"

"It means that Jesse knows that he owes us plenty and I'm sure he's not the kind of man who could let that debt go unpaid."

"So we're stuck with a loose cannon . . . a stranger who has a famous killer for an uncle and whom we know nothing about?"

"Looks like," Longarm told her.

"Heaven help us! It's not as if we don't have enough to worry about with Joe Bean."

Longarm placed a hand on her shoulder. "Sometimes good things come in bad packages, Lizzy. I'm thinking that Jesse Horn is going to prove to be a blessing in disguise."

"For an ex-lawman, you're extremely trusting."

"No," Longarm countered, "I'm not. What I am is a very good judge of character and I think Jesse has character in spades."

"For our sakes, I hope you're right."

"Me, too," Longarm said as he took the money she was offering and said good-bye. "Come along as soon as you can, Lizzy."

"Don't worry. I won't stay a minute longer than is necessary to get that girl up and moving to our ranch. Just watch your back, Custis."

"Should I watch it for Jesse . . . or Joe Bean?"

"Sadly, maybe *both*," Lizzy said before turning back to the unconscious young woman.

Longarm and Jesse gathered their belongings and headed for the stagecoach office. When they arrived, it was almost nine o'clock and there were four other people waiting on board.

"Looks like you have a full load to Salida," Longarm told the driver.

"Sure do!" the man said, leaning close and whispering. "To tell you the truth, I think that most of them are going there just so they can sit beside you and the cowboy and hear all about what happened up in the hotel room last night. We haven't had that kind of a shoot-up for more than two years!"

Longarm scowled. "Well," he said, "we're not talking about what happened, so you might as well go tell those folks to get off the stagecoach right now."

"And give them back their money? Not a chance! This line needs every paying passenger it can get or I'll be laid off and out of work."

"Life is tough," Longarm said without a hint of sympathy.

"That young cowboy sure looks bad with those stitches on his face."

"He'll mend."

"I got to see the gambler's body over at the mortuary. It was laid out on a slab for everyone to view, but it cost a nickel."

"The undertaker charged people a nickel to see that dead man?"

"Sure did! And he'd stripped the gambler down to the waist and showed us where all six bullets went in and where three of 'em went back out. I tell you, that was some shooting!"

"Yeah," Longarm said, his mood soured even more by this conversation than he'd thought possible.

"I heard tell that that kid is Tom Horn's kid."

"I don't think so," Longarm said, just wanting to get on board and leave this town.

"Well," the driver said, opening the door to reveal a bunch of morbidly curious passengers, "he sure is a gunslinger, by Gawd!"

Jesse heard that and said in anger, "I ain't no gunslinger, you foolish sonofabitch!"

The driver paled and threw his hands up in self-defense. "Don't get mad and shoot me, Mr. Horn! I . . . I didn't mean any insult. Honest!"

Jesse shook his head with disgust and said, "I'm riding up on top. I think the air in this coach is foul."

"I agree," Longarm said, helping the wounded cowboy up and then following him to sit on the coach.

The driver looked aggrieved and disappointed. But he was too intimidated by Jesse to protest them sitting on his coach, so he climbed up into the box and they headed off to Salida.

Chapter 10

Salida was a beautiful mountain town near the headwaters of the Arkansas River. Situated at just over seven thousand feet in elevation, it had a reputation for having one of the mildest winters in Colorado's high country, and with the Arkansas River flowing through its wide grassy valley, it was a perfect setting for cattle ranching.

The town itself was small, but it appeared to be prosperous and growing. Everywhere Longarm looked, he saw new buildings under construction.

"I could use a beer," Jesse Horn said as they departed the stagecoach. "I've still got a hangover from last night."

"I'm surprised that you even remember what happened up in that room," Longarm said. "You and Teresa drank a full bottle of whiskey."

"Yeah, we did," Jesse admitted. "I'm surprised my aim was so good given all that liquor."

"Maybe you got a little lucky," Longarm told the young cowboy.

"Maybe," Jesse conceded, "but Clyde was standing right there in the doorway and he was illuminated by the hallway lamps. Teresa and I, on the other hand, had been sleeping in a shadowy corner of that hotel room. So I really had a lot better look at him than he had of us."

"Even so," Longarm said, "he shot Teresa three times."

"If she dies, I'm never gonna forgive myself," Jesse said with a sad shake of his head. "I didn't know her very long, but what little time we had together was pretty special."

"Are you serious, or is that just bullshit?"

"No! I'm serious!" Jesse looked aggrieved. "I really meant it when I said I'd take her all the way to California someday. Why, I figure they must need working cowboys in California. Don't you think?"

"I suppose," Longarm said, not much interested.

But Jesse didn't want to drop the subject. "I heard that they have those Mexican vaqueros that can really ride and rope," he said, looking to the northwest where Mt. Shavano, glistening with a deep mantle of snow, towered over fourteen thousand feet into the sky.

"I expect there are quite a few good cowboys in this neck of the woods," Longarm agreed. "We saw some real nice cattle ranches coming in on the stagecoach today."

"This is fine cattle-raising country," Jesse said, sounding more enthused. "Plenty of grass and water. I expected that the snow gets deep up here, but it's nearly melted off already. I'm mighty glad to see that."

"Me, too," Longarm said. "And while I'd also like a beer, I think we'd better start buying some food and outfitting ourselves for the ride to Lizzy's ranch."

"Kinda late in the day already," Jesse mused, glancing up at the sun now low in the western horizon. "By the time we get the supplies, horses, saddles, and all bought, it's gonna be awful late in the day. It's never a good idea to ride out lookin' for a ranch in the dark."

"Maybe not," Longarm replied, "but that's exactly what we're going to do. The way you get into trouble, I'm thinking that the sooner we get out of this town, the better all around."

"Aw," Jesse said, "I don't usually get into fights and shoot people when I'm staying in a town."

"Nice to hear that," Longarm said cryptically. "But all the same, I am anxious to see the ranch. And there's a full moon out tonight, so we shouldn't have any trouble keeping to the roads."

"You're the boss," Jesse said, looking disappointed. "But when a man is in a hurry to buy horses and such, he usually gets skinned."

"Are you a good horse trader?"

Jesse nodded. "Sure am."

"Then I'll let you pick our horses and haggle over the prices. How's that sound?"

"Sounds like a good idea," Jesse replied, brightened. "I know and love horses almost as well as I know and love women. I'll also be buyin' a couple of saddles and some blankets, bridles, halters, and such as we'll need."

"Keep your spending to a minimum," Longarm told the cowboy. "Most likely, there are saddles and tack at the ranch. No sense in spending money that we don't have to spend. I'd rather put the money on things we'll need after we take inventory and see what the ranch is lacking."

"If it doesn't have horses or cattle, I'd say it's lacking about everything you have to have on a ranch," Jesse told him.

"Just don't spend much money on our horses and saddles," Longarm told him. "And while you're doing that, I'll hike down to that general store and buy a few days worth of provisions."

"Buy us a little whiskey, and I wouldn't mind a cigar or at least some tobacco and the makin's."

"I'll see about that," Longarm answered, leaving the cowboy and heading for the general store.

An hour later, Longarm had filled his modest order for provisions and had it all stuffed into a cotton sack that he could tie on to his saddle. He didn't much like spending Lizzy's money . . . it just didn't sit well with him, so he used some of his own dwindling funds.

When he arrived at the stable, Jesse was saddling a blue roan gelding while another man was saddling an ugly little pinto.

Longarm was no cowboy, and he had never claimed to be a good judge of horseflesh, but he wasn't completely ignorant when it came to horses.

"You bought these two ugly horses?" he asked in amazement.

"Sure did," Jesse said. "Got 'em for only forty dollars."

"Each?"

"No, for the pair."

"He skinned me alive," the stable owner said, finishing saddling the pinto. The man was a thin fellow wearing filthy bib overalls, with no shirt or shoes, and chewing on a plug of tobacco, which caused him to spit constantly. "I never saw such a tough man to deal with as Jesse."

"Jesse, I never seen two sorrier horses than these," Longarm complained. "Why, they're just a couple of big-headed runts!"

"Oh," Jesse said, dropping the stirrup after tightening the cinch to his satisfaction. "You may be right about this pair not being tall and flashy, but I got an eye for quality and even though they ain't real beauties, they're stout and I'm betting anything they're damned fast."

"What makes you think so?" Longarm said, still skeptical.

"I rode both of 'em."

"You did?"

"Sure!" Jesse grinned. "Rode 'em both bareback around and around the barn and out toward that river. The blue, he bucked me off, but I got right back on and kicked him in the guts and he found some manners. And the pinto, he tried to bite my hand off, but I punched him in the eye, bit down, and then twisted his ear around about four times, and he become an instant gentleman."

Longarm just stared at the cowboy and then at the ugly pair of geldings with the feeling that he should have done the horse buying himself.

"Jesse did ride hell outa 'em both," the stable owner said. "This cowboy sure gave these two ponies some God-fearing religion! Why, I've had quite a few cowboys try to ride them and none of 'em stuck."

"Great," Longarm said. "But I'm not a cowboy and I don't want to fight with a damned horse every time I get near him."

"I'll handle that," Jesse said with absolute assurance. "Don't you worry, Custis, I won't let these ponies hurt you none."

Longarm surveyed a corral of horses. "How about we let you have those two and I buy a . . . a better-mannered and taller animal? I like the looks of that tall sorrel."

The stable owner beamed. "Why, mister, now you're talking about a fine animal! That sorrel is the handsomest horse in the pen. He's only four years old and broke for a kid to ride."

"How much do you want for the horse?" Longarm asked.

"Forty dollars."

"Just for him?"

"That's right," the stable owner said, "and he's worth twice that much. Only reason I'd sell him for forty dollars is that you're buyin' quantity here. It'll only cost you forty dollars for the two runts that the cowboy gave religion, forty for the sorrel, and another forty for two saddles, bridles, and blankets. Comes to only a hundred-twenty dollars total in cash! Mister, that's one hell of a good deal."

Longarm hooked his thumbs into his belt and thought about it for a moment, then reluctantly decided he didn't want to spend that much of Lizzy's money or any more of

93

his own. "Jesse? Are you sure that those two runts are going to turn out to be good ranch horses?"

"I'm as sure as I am that the sun will rise tomorrow morning."

"All right, then," Longarm reluctantly concluded. "Which one do I have to ride?"

"Take your pick!" Jesse was grinning from ear to ear.

"No, I want the one least likely to kill me," Longarm said stubbornly.

"Okay. You can ride the blue roan. I'll ride the pinto just in case he's already forgotten about me biting and then corkscrewing his ear."

Longarm was getting impatient and the sun was almost ready to set. "Good enough. Let's get to traveling."

"Mister," the stable owner said, making one more try at selling a third horse, "I sure think that you ought to buy that handsome sorrel. You look like a man who values your life and health and I'd hate to see you get hurt on that blue roan."

"I'm going to take my chances," Longarm said. "If he doesn't work out in the next day or two, I'll come back and trade him in for the sorrel."

The stable owner spat on the ground and toed dirt. "Mister, I'm afraid that would cost you more than I'm offerin' right now."

Longarm poked the stable owner in the chest with his stiff forefinger. "You'll buy the roan back at twenty dollars and sell me the sorrel for forty and that will be the deal or I'll kick your ass all around your run-down barn. Is that clearly understood?"

The stable owner wasn't a small man, but he wasn't any match for Longarm, so he nodded and spat a stream of dark tobacco juice at a passing rooster. "No reason for you to get nasty about it, mister."

"Just tell me where the Holden Ranch is to be found."

"You mean the Lazy H?"

"I mean the one that Miss Lizzy Holden and her father own."

"Why, the old man is dead."

"Lizzy Holden isn't dead and I'm the new half-owner of the ranch, so where the hell is it?" Longarm demanded, his patience at the breaking point.

The stable owner gaped and spat again. "*You're* the new half-owner?"

Longarm reached out and grabbed the man by the shirtfront. "Where is the damned ranch!"

"Six miles north of here! Follow the road until it forks about three miles out, then take the right fork and you'll soon be on the ranch itself. The house is back in the trees under a low bluff. Pretty a place as you'll ever find and you can't miss it, mister . . ."

"Custis Long. And the cowboy's name is Jesse Horn."

"Oh, I know his name." The man batted Longarm's hand away and chewed fast on his plug. "That cowboy is Tom Horn's *son.*"

Longarm shot a glance at Jesse, then back at the livery owner. "Is that what he's telling people now?"

"That's what he told me," the stable owner said, turning a suspicious eye on Jesse. "Ain't he?"

"I believe he is," Longarm said, not wanting to trap Jesse in a bald-faced lie.

"When I heard that, I knew that I had to give him a real good deal or his pa might come here and shoot me plumb full of bullet holes."

"I understand," Longarm said. He tied the sack of newly bought provisions to his battered saddle. Then he cautiously mounted the roan, half-expecting to be tossed.

But the stout and ugly blue didn't move a muscle. Longarm sat up straight and tall in the saddle and breathed a quiet sigh of relief. "Jesse," he said, "let's get moving. It'll be dark in less than an hour."

"If it's only six miles to the Lazy H, on these fast

95

ponies we can be there in less than half an hour," Jesse promised.

"Maybe we could be, but we won't be," Longarm said. "I got a sack of provisions tied to my saddle and I won't be beat to death by canned goods. So let's set out at the trot and get there in forty-five minutes."

"Okay," Jesse said, "whatever you say, Boss."

Longarm put his heels to the blue. All of a sudden, the beast dropped its big, jug head and started bucking like he had nettles under his saddle blanket. The cotton sack of provisions broke apart and the next thing that Longarm knew, he and all the tins of food and supplies were sailing into the sky in every direction. Longarm hit the ground like a ton of bricks and groaned while the roan bucked to a standstill, then turned its ugly head and watched to see what he would do next.

"Damn you, Jesse!" Longarm shouted when he managed to get air back into his lungs. "I thought you told me you had taught that horse some manners!"

"Sorry, Boss." Jesse was trying not to laugh. "You can ride the pinto. I'll ride the blue."

"No!" Longarm shouted, slowly picking himself off the ground. "Pick up everything and cram it back in the sack."

"That sack is split open and won't hold those cans and stuff anymore," the stable owner observed, also looking quite proud of the blue roan. "But I'll sell you a good burlap feed sack for a dollar."

Longarm wanted to draw his gun and shoot the blue roan and then the stable owner and finally Jesse Horn. Instead, he bellowed, "All right, I'll buy the sorrel gelding, dammit! And for one hundred twenty dollars you'd better throw in a third saddle!"

The stable owner started to protest the deal. To haggle. But when he looked into Longarm's eyes, he had a sudden change of heart and nodded in wise agreement.

"Mister, those three horses and saddles and a burlap

bag will tally up to one hundred twenty-one dollars, and you're getting the best deal I ever gave an angry, ill-tempered man."

Longarm gave him the money and ground his teeth in silent fury while the stable owner found another old saddle and put it on the handsome sorrel gelding. When the horse was bridled, Longarm mounted the animal and found it to be as gentle and well-mannered as promised.

"You'll be coming back here to buy some more horses for your ranch," the stable owner called as they rode out of Salida. "Don't forget how I gave you the best deal of a life-time with those three fine animals and saddles!"

Longarm twisted around in the saddle and felt a sharp stab of pain in his backside where he'd hit the ground so hard. He gave the stable owner a hand gesture that left no doubt about his feelings toward the man.

"Ah," Jesse said, "you didn't need to go and do that. He was a pretty good old boy."

"He was nearly the death of me," Longarm groused. "And so were you, for that matter."

"We'll need all three horses anyway," the cowboy figured. "Don't you worry about that. I'll be usin' the blue and this pinto pretty hard. And don't forget that Miss Lizzy is going to need her own horse."

"Well, she's certainly not going to want to ride either the blue or the pinto."

"I hope not," Jesse said seriously. "But I'll get her another good deal on a horse when she comes to town. Maybe she'll even want me to buy a horse for Teresa O'Connell."

Longarm shook his head. It was going to be a long six miles riding to the Lazy H with this idiot cowboy.

Chapter 11

Longarm raised his hand and pointed. "That must be the Lazy H ranch house and barns."

Jesse reined in his horse and stared. "From the light I can see coming from the windows, someone must be living at the ranch."

"Lizzy told me that the house is supposed to be empty," Longarm said.

"Do you think Joe Bean might be staking his claim on the ranch?"

Longarm shook his head. "I doubt it. Joe would realize that I'm coming here and he wouldn't want to give me any advance warning. I don't know who could be holed up in Lizzy's ranch house."

"Guess we're going to find out soon enough," Jesse said. "One thing I do know is that I'm mighty cold and I'm hungry and nobody is turning us away tonight."

"You got that right," Longarm replied. "Jesse, it probably wouldn't be a bad idea for us to separate and ride in from opposite angles. Whoever is inside Lizzy's place tonight might not be friendly."

"Good idea," Jesse said. "We're pretty easy targets given all this moonlight."

"Just don't start shooting unless whoever is in there opens fire on us," Longarm warned. "If he's someone hired by Joe Bean to put up opposition, I want to know about it and then what else he's up to."

Jesse glanced up at the full moon. "A little while ago I was grateful for the moonlight, and now I'm wishing a cloud would pass over that moon and give us some cover."

Longarm reined up the sorrel and dismounted. He had the fine shotgun and he made sure it was loaded. "I think I'll walk the rest of the way up to the ranch."

"Sounds like the wise thing to do," Jesse replied, also dismounting and then leading his two horses away.

Longarm didn't know what to expect as he neared the ranch while leading the sorrel, but past experience had taught him to always expect the very worst. When he got to about a hundred yards from the house, two big ranch dogs jumped up from under the porch and started barking furiously. Longarm had faced guard dogs before and he could tell this pair was ferocious. Attacking dogs were almost impossible to shoot under the most ideal circumstances, so he grabbed a handful of shotgun shells from his supply bag and dumped them in his coat pockets. If the dogs came at him in a rush, he would blow them to bloody bits.

Almost immediately, the light from inside the ranch house was extinguished and the curtains drawn. Longarm knew that he and Jesse were no longer going to own the element of surprise.

A crack in the front door opened and a man with a rifle shouted, "Who goes out there sneakin' around in the dark!"

"I'm a friend of Miss Holden's. Who are you and what are you doing in that house? You're trespassing!"

There was a moment of silence, and then the man in the doorway swore and opened fire on Longarm. His first rifle bullet clipped the horn of Longarm's saddle, and the second bullet skinned the sorrel gelding's shoulder and sent it rearing over backward. The animal was hurt and wild with pain. It tore loose from Longarm's grasp, got up, and went galloping off into the night.

Longarm dropped to the ground where he was no longer a clear or easy target. Because the man in the doorway was out of the shotgun's effective killing range, he yanked out his six-gun and returned fire. The door slammed shut, and then two rifles busted windowpanes in the front of the house and belched flames.

Well, Longarm thought, *at least I've learned that there is more than one of them in the house.*

One of the men inside was shooting at Jesse Horn, who was dragging his horses toward a line of cottonwood trees fed by a valley stream. Longarm saw Jesse and the horses make the trees and the badly needed cover.

The men inside fired into the cottonwoods, but Jesse wasn't firing back. Most likely, he was tying the geldings up where they would be out of harm's way, and then he would start working his way toward the ranch house.

Longarm, however, wasn't so fortunate. He was out in the open and there was absolutely no cover to hide behind or use to help him get closer to the house.

The firing stopped and the rifle barrels disappeared from the broken windows. Longarm figured that the pair . . . or maybe there were even more than two . . . were reloading and sizing up their situation.

It was time to move even without cover. Otherwise, he would be lying on flat ground and going nowhere all night. And with dawn, Longarm knew that he'd make an easy target. Picking up the shotgun and taking a deep breath, Longarm took off running hard and fast toward Lizzy's big hay barn. He was almost there when the two barking ranch dogs flew off the porch and came racing at him with rumbles in their throats and their long fangs white and glistening with saliva.

They were big and they were killers. Before Longarm could reach the barn, one of the mongrels clamped his jaws on Longarm's boot top and the other went right for his throat. Longarm fell and rolled. When he came up, he lashed out with the shotgun and struck one of the dogs in the face. It yelped in pain and backed up for a moment, shaking its head and growling. Having no other choice, Longarm unleashed one of the loads in his shotgun; the vicious mongrel's entire head disappeared. The second dog saw what happened to its companion and instantly forgot about tearing Longarm's leg to pieces. It let out a howl and took off running back toward the ranch house with its tail tucked between its legs. Longarm raised the shotgun and considered blowing the dog's ass off, but he changed his mind and let the animal disappear under the front porch, where it continued to howl in abject horror.

A bullet struck the dirt in front of Longarm, and it sent him racing toward the barn, which he made without getting killed.

"Custis, are you all right!" came Jesse's voice from the cottonwoods.

"I'm all right," Custis shouted. "Let's move in and get 'em!"

Longarm was now close enough to bring the shotgun into play. Even if it didn't actually have the range to penetrate the ranch house or kill the men inside, it would certainly catch their attention and put cold, paralyzing fear into their hearts. He fired two more loads at the house and started advancing.

Jesse also opened fire. Longarm saw the cowboy's muzzle fire, and realized that Jesse was much closer than expected. The men inside began to return fire, and Longarm drew his six-gun. He waited until one of the riflemen lingered a second too long in the window, and sent a bullet straight into his body.

Longarm heard a scream, and then he heard Jesse yell something and start charging toward the house.

102

"Don't shoot! I give up!" the man in the house cried. "Don't shoot anymore!"

To back up his plea, a rifle sailed through the front window. Longarm holstered his six-gun and reloaded both barrels of the shotgun.

"Jesse!" Longarm shouted, leaving the cover of the barn and hurrying across the yard. "Don't . . ."

Jesse was running hard toward the house and the blood was pounding in his ears so that he couldn't hear the man's surrender. When his boot struck the porch, he ducked his head and went flying straight through the already shattered window with both guns blazing.

"Damn!" Longarm swore as he charged up the porch and into the house with his shotgun reloaded and ready to kill anyone lurking inside.

Jesse climbed off the living room floor with a badly cut hand. "We got 'em both, Custis."

The light inside was poor, but Longarm could see two dead men lying sprawled on Lizzy's floor. He looked around and spotted a kerosene lamp. Moments later, he was staring at the two dead men while listening to the terrified mongrel still howling and carrying on under the porch.

"I think I'll shoot that dog," Jesse said, starting to go outside. "I can't stand to hear the damned thing wail over and over."

"Leave the dog alone. He'll settle down soon enough."

"He'd better," Jesse warned. "I won't stand listening to him for long."

"I had to blow the other dog's head clean away," Longarm told the cowboy.

Jesse was more interested in the two dead men than he was in a dog. "Who do you think these two jaspers were?"

"I don't know," Longarm said with a trace of bitterness. "But didn't you hear one yelling that he was surrendering? He even tossed this rifle through the window."

"I was breathing hard and running even harder with my gun talking as fast as I could squeeze the trigger," Jesse explained. "So I didn't hear anyone surrendering."

"Well," Longarm said, miffed that he had no prisoners to interrogate. "The bigger one tried to give up, and I sure wish we could have taken him alive and learned what he and his friend were doing here."

"Most likely, they were drifters who found a nice, empty ranch house and decided to take up permanent residence and fight to keep it."

"Maybe," Longarm said. "Or they might have been hired by Joe Bean to lie in wait and capture Lizzy."

"Guess we'll never know."

Longarm surveyed the living room. "What an unholy, stinking mess," he said, shaking his head. "I'm glad that Lizzy isn't here with us now . . . she'd be devastated to see her house looking like a hog's pen."

"They *were* hogs," Jesse said, taking in all the trash, and now smelling rotting food and garbage that were fouling up the kitchen. "It'll take a day or two to clean up and ventilate this place."

"We'll have to find a hammer and nails to tack blankets over those two front windows that were busted and shot out," Longarm said. "But first let's drag these bodies out on the porch. They're bleeding all over the floor."

"Two dead men on the porch bleeding through the planks onto that crazed dog underneath sure won't calm his nerves."

"Leave the dog alone. I feel bad enough about what I did to the other one. After all, he was just doing what he had been trained to do."

"I like horses and don't like dogs much," Jesse announced. "It'd be better to put that other one out of his misery since he sounds like he's lost his mind."

"Let's search the bodies and then Lizzy's house and see what we learn. Maybe there's evidence that the pair we shot were hired by Joe Bean."

"Maybe," Jesse said, bending down and starting to search the pockets of one dead man while Longarm searched the other man's clothes.

"Nothing," Longarm said after a few minutes. "But that doesn't mean they didn't have belongings and we'll probably find them in the bedrooms."

"They sure do smell bad," Jesse said, grabbing the arms of one of the men and dragging him outside on the porch. "Shut up, dog!"

The dog didn't shut up, but instead kept howling. Jesse dropped the man's arms and grabbed his gun. He fired at the porch hoping to hit the crazed dog, but his gun was empty.

"Don't," Longarm said. "Just leave him be to settle down."

"You got to kill a dog tonight, why shouldn't I get to do the same?"

"Because the dog under our feet isn't any danger."

Jesse reloaded, then holstered his gun and stomped back into the house. "At least there is a fire going and plenty of split wood to burn. Let's get these windows covered up and the door closed before this place gets cold with the night air."

Longarm said, "You take care of that and then go find my sorrel gelding that was wounded and ran away with our supplies. In the meantime, I'll search the house and see if I can find out who those two were and what they were doing living in the house."

"Custis, my guess is that they were just down-and-out drifters," Jesse said. "They probably thought they'd found an ideal place to winter and maybe even settle onto for good. That was their big mistake."

"Yeah," Longarm said, heading off to find the bedrooms and hoping that the two men hadn't destroyed all of Lizzy and her father's most prized family possessions, "their big and *fatal* mistake."

Chapter 12

They never found even a scrap of information about the two dead squatters, not even their names, much less a connection to Joe Bean. After burying the unnamed pair in unmarked graves out on the range, Longarm and Jesse spent three hard days cleaning up Lizzy's ranch house and taking an inventory of what was there and what they would need to buy.

"The weather is holding good," Jesse said as they sat before the fireplace sipping a little whiskey after a supper of beef and beans. "Did Miss Holden really sell *all* of her cattle?"

"Yep," Longarm answered, "at least that's what I understood her to say."

Jesse yawned and got up to stretch. "In the morning, I'm going to saddle the blue roan and ride our fence lines. I'll also take the pinto and some food and a bedroll. I want to cover every square foot of this ranch and make sure that there are no Lazy H horses or cattle to be found. I also need to check the fence line for any breaks. No sense in us buying replacement stock if they can walk off the ranch onto someone else's place."

"That makes a lot of sense to me," Longarm said in

agreement. "I did find some Lazy H branding irons out in the barn."

"We'll need them when we buy new stock." Jesse smiled and sipped at his whiskey. "Custis, I have to know if you've ever branded cattle or horses."

"Can't say as I have."

"Good time to learn and I'm an excellent teacher," Jesse said. "Can you rope?"

"Nope," Longarm answered. "I never even owned one. The only kind of rope I have any experience with is a hangman's rope."

Jesse frowned. "Now that *is* a problem. You see, Boss, you can't brand a cow or calf unless you first catch it."

"Well," Longarm replied, "then I hope you're one helluva good roper."

"As a matter of fact, I am."

"You ever pulled a calf?" Jesse asked.

Longarm scowled. "Pulled it from *what*? A muddy bog?"

"No. From its mammy."

"I've never even seen it happen," Longarm told the cowboy, not even trying to imagine how bloody and disgusting that would be. "And I don't believe that I care to do it anyway."

"Well, hell's fire, Custis, if a calf gets turned wrong inside its mother, say it wants to come out sideways . . ."

"Whoa!" Longarm shouted, downing his whiskey. "Would a calf actually try to do that?"

"Sure!" Jesse shook his head in amazement at Longarm's lack of knowledge. "I mean, it's not like the calf wants to come out sideways, but sometimes it just doesn't get turned right, and then you have to reach up into the momma cow and turn it around and pull it out."

"Shit," Longarm said, shaking his head. "I'd rather shoot the cow for having a sideways calf and go on to the next cow."

"Man, you can't do that!" Jesse exclaimed. "A rancher or cowman's first responsibility is *always* to his livestock."

"Well," Longarm said, "then I guess I'm going to make a damn poor rancher. Because, truth be told, my first responsibility is going to be to protect Lizzy and myself from Joe Bean. After that comes taking care of this place and the horses. The cows will come near the bottom of my list."

Jesse couldn't believe what he was hearing. "You sure got a lot of mind adjustments to make," Jesse said with a worried expression. "If you think like that, you'll never cut the mustard as a rancher."

Longarm bristled. "Listen, I've been 'cutting the mustard' for a good long while, and I'm not too worried that I'm going to come up short. At least not in terms of handling the big problems that will come with this ranch."

"It's a fine ranch," Jesse said, "and that's a fact. Do you fully realize how lucky you are to have fallen into this deal?"

Longarm almost decided not to answer that impertinent question, but he changed his mind. "Jesse, it's true that I'm getting half-ownership in this spread . . . but only if I decide that's the life I want to lead. And right now, I'm a long way from reaching that conclusion."

"Meaning?"

"Meaning I told Lizzy that I'd give this a go and see if it will work between us. If not, then I'll leave here without a backward glance."

Jesse was amazed. "You'd just walk away from a sweet deal like getting a fine woman and a damn valuable ranch?"

"You bet I would," Longarm told the dumbfounded cowboy. "Life is far too short to be stuck doing something that you're either not any good at or don't give two damns about."

"Most men would kill for the setup you're walking into."

"I'm not most men." Longarm studied Jesse Horn

across the firelight. "And I hope you're not the kind to kill for this place."

"No, I'm not," Jesse said, looking Longarm straight in the eyes.

"But killing seems to come easy for you, doesn't it." Longarm wasn't asking a question, he was stating a proven fact.

"I suppose it does," Jesse admitted. "My uncle Tom has probably killed a dozen men or more. Indians. Mexicans. White men. He's killed a bunch of all of 'em, so maybe killing is something that comes natural to a family named Horn."

Longarm considered that statement for several minutes and then he said, "I wish you hadn't killed the one that surrendered. He never deserved to die. Probably was just a drifter like you thought."

"When he opened fire on us," Jesse said, "he and the other one signed their death warrants."

Longarm tossed his cheroot into the fireplace. "When you ride out tomorrow, I'm going to saddle up the sorrel and go back into Salida. We need some more provisions and I want to post a letter to Lizzy asking her how soon she thinks she can get here. I don't feel comfortable spending her money without getting her opinion first."

"Just be sure and ask her how Miss O'Connell is recovering," Jesse said. "I'm anxious to see that girl again."

"I'll do that," Longarm promised.

Jesse stood up and yawned. "Are you sure it's a good idea for both of us to leave this ranch house at the same time?"

Longarm had already considered that risk. "It probably isn't, but I won't be gone but a few hours at the most."

"Good," Jesse said. "Just watch out for that Joe Bean fella. He might be hanging around out there someplace waiting for us to separate so he can slip into this house and ambush us when we return."

"He might be at that," Longarm agreed.

"I'll keep a close watch for tracks," Jesse promised. "If Bean or anyone else has been out here spying on this place, they'll have had to have left some tracks and I'll not miss 'em."

"Good night," Longarm said, heading for Lizzy's bedroom.

"I'll be gone before first morning light. I'll be back the day after tomorrow knowing if there are any Lazy H horses or cattle on the place."

"I don't expect there will be."

"You can never tell," Jesse said, disappearing. "Sometimes stock get pretty good at hiding come roundup time. You ever even been on a cattle roundup, Custis?"

Longarm didn't even bother to answer as he went to prepare to sleep.

Chapter 13

"Your color is much improved today," the doctor said after changing Teresa O'Connell's bandages. "And your wounds are healing nicely. I'm happy to say that you're mending much faster than I'd even dared to hope."

Teresa smiled and glanced over toward Lizzy. "I've had excellent nursing from my new and best friend."

Lizzy blushed with pride. "Teresa, you're a good and uncomplaining patient."

Teresa returned her attention back to the doctor. "How much longer will I have to stay in bed?"

"Oh," he mused, "I'd say no more than another day."

"I was hoping to be allowed to at least get up and use the bathroom down the hallway on my own."

"I'm afraid that's a little too ambitious," the doctor said. "However, I think it would be all right if you wanted to get out of bed and sit in a chair for part of the day. But you'd have to move very slowly and carefully. Your wounds are still a long way from being fully healed and we don't want to run the risk of them tearing open."

Teresa was wildly impatient to get out of bed and move around. "But, Doctor, I feel plenty strong enough to walk."

"Then let's see if we can help you get up and sit in that chair across the room."

Teresa brightened. "All right."

"But very slowly and only with our help."

Teresa waited until her covers were removed, and then she allowed her feet to be slid off the bed and onto the floor. A moment later, with the doctor on one arm and Lizzy on the other supporting most of her weight, Teresa stood and slowly shuffled across the hotel room to a chair.

"Easy," the doctor said, helping her to sit down. "That's the way of it. How do you feel?"

"I feel like I could go for a walk from one end of Buena Vista to the other," Teresa responded. "I feel terrific!"

"Let's just keep you feeling that way," the doctor said. "Walk a little farther each day back and forth across this room. If you make as much progress next week as you have this past week, I think you will be fit to travel to Salida."

"I can't wait!" Teresa gushed.

"Neither can I," Lizzy said. "I just received a letter from Custis, and he says that everything is going well and that he and Jesse are eager for us to join them at the Lazy H."

"I'm not going to be holding you up much longer," Teresa promised. "In fact, if you wanted to, Lizzy, you could go on and I could follow you to the ranch in a few days."

"No," Lizzy said emphatically. "I'm not leaving until you are able to climb onto a stagecoach and go with me."

"I agree fully with that decision," the doctor said. "However, given the remarkable way this girl is recovering, I should think that you ought to be able to leave this hotel and go to your ranch in about a week."

Lizzy nodded, although she secretly wondered how she could stay away from Custis Long and the Lazy H that much longer.

"All right," the doctor said, packing his medical supplies back in his satchel and preparing to go. "Now, Miss

O'Connell, I'm not leaving you any more pain medicine since you say you're not experiencing much pain."

"I'm not," Teresa assured him.

"Very well, then. I'll see you tomorrow."

When the doctor was gone, Lizzy and Teresa happily discussed how glad they were about the doctor's optimistic prognosis. "You'll love the Lazy H," Lizzy promised.

"I'm sure that I will," Teresa said. "And I sure do want to see Jesse again as soon as possible."

Lizzy nodded. "I should go out and buy some fresh bandages and a few things we need."

"Go ahead," Teresa told her, still sitting in the chair dressed in her nightgown. "I'll be all right."

"Don't try to get up and move before I come back. You could fall and reopen the wounds."

"I won't."

"Promise?" Lizzy asked.

"I promise. There's a magazine on the table. Could you please get it for me?"

"Of course. I won't be gone more than an hour."

"I'll be sitting here reading when you return," Teresa said.

When Lizzy left, she locked the door, satisfied that her patient would be just fine.

After perhaps a half hour, Teresa O'Connell suddenly had a terribly strong urge to go to the bathroom. Her chamber pot was pushed well under the bed, and it would hurt more to get on the floor and try to retrieve it than it would to slowly and carefully shuffle down the hallway to the toilet at the end of the hallway.

Setting her magazine on the side table, Teresa slowly pushed herself to her feet and shuffled across the room to the door. She unlocked it and poked her head out into the hallway, which was empty. Satisfied that she would not be seen by anyone and feeling no pain or dizziness, she closed the door behind her and moved purposefully to the little bathroom at the end of the hallway, wondering if she should confess this act to Lizzy.

She decided that she ought not to say anything to her about this forbidden outing, and besides, when you really had to go, you *really* had to go!

Teresa was relieved to find that the little bathroom at the end of the hall was not occupied. She did her business with a sigh of relief and washed herself in the sink using a clean towel provided by the hotel.

"I really could go downstairs and walk around this town for a little while," she said to herself with growing confidence. "The doctor is being much too cautious. But I'll behave and follow their orders. I'm so grateful to have such a good doctor and friend taking care of me."

Teresa closed the door and hurriedly shuffled along on the carpet to her room, feeling a little guilty for her secret excursion, but also quite proud of herself for exceeding her doctor's best expectations.

She slipped back inside their hotel room and locked the door. She would go back to the chair and say nary a word to Lizzy about this outing. It would be her little secret.

"Thanks for locking the door," a voice said as Teresa turned. "Saves me the trouble."

Cold fear flooded Teresa O'Connell's now empty bowels, and she staggered and grabbed for the door handle, but Joe Bean was already at her side. His hand was like a vise when it clamped onto her wrist and his voice was soft, but that somehow made it all the more menacing.

"Let me help you back to bed," he told her with a cold smile. "You're still very weak, Miss O'Connell."

"No!" she cried, noticing for the first time that there was another man in her room. A big man with red hair and pale blue eyes. "Let go of me! Get out of this room! Both of you!"

But Joe Bean didn't seem to be listening. He nodded to

the big, hulking man who had been sitting in the chair that Teresa had most recently vacated. The redheaded man came out of the chair and scooped Teresa up as if she were a rag doll, then carried her to the bed. She tried to beat at his beard and gouge his eyes, but he slammed his forehead into her head with such force that she lost consciousness.

"Put her to bed and stay away from her while I'm gone," Joe Bean warned.

The giant scowled. "I only want to use her for a few minutes. Dammit, Joe, she's real pretty and she won't even know what happened."

"She'd know," Joe said. "And then I'd know and I'd have to kill you for disobeying my orders. Is screwing an unconscious woman worth losing your life over, Bert?"

Bert's lower lip jutted out in defiance. "I sure don't see what the big deal is about her."

"I told you that I need you standing by the window watching for my signal from down in the street. I intend to intercept Miss Holden as she leaves the mercantile and before she returns to this hotel. I want her to see you standing in her hotel window after I explain exactly what I have in mind for her and Custis Long."

"Okay," Bert said with heavy reluctance. "And after that I could . . ."

"Goddamn you, leave her *alone*!"

Bert's eyes were set deep under a massive ridge of sloping forehead. His nose was flattened, his face pocked and scarred from many barroom brawls. He stood six-foot-four and weighed 250 pounds and not one ounce of it was fat.

"I got a powerful hunger for her body," Bert breathed, eyes hot with desire.

"You can have her later," Joe Bean said, leaving the room. "After it's all over. Hell, Bert, if everything goes according to my plan, you can have Miss O'Connell as long as she can stand up to your pounding."

Bert guffawed. When Joe Bean left the room, Bert

walked over to the bed and stared down at the unconscious young beauty. His hands were thick and heavy, and he used them to quickly examine Teresa's most secret and private parts.

"Hot, young, and juicy," he said with almost childlike glee.

Bert towered over the semiconscious and exposed Teresa. He drooled, mouth slack with desire. He licked his fat lips and then vigorously rubbed his crotch until he began to stiffen. He'd wait to have this woman, but he wouldn't wait for very damned long.

Chapter 14

"Good morning, Miss Holden!" a cheerful voice called out. "May I help you carry those bags up to your hotel room this morning?"

Lizzy twisted around on the boardwalk and gasped. "Joe Bean! What . . . what are you doing here?"

"Why, I have important business here in Buena Vista," he said, tipping his hat like a gentleman.

Lizzy's stomach bound up in a hard knot. "*You're* the one who murdered my father, aren't you!"

His smile slipped, but only a little. "Why, of course not! And I'm real sorry I wasn't able to find out who did murder your father. But rest assured that I haven't given up yet, so your thousand-dollar fee is still in effect."

"Get away from me!" Lizzy hissed, taking a back step. "Even better, leave the state and never return."

Joe Bean rocked back on his boot heels, looking surprised and hurt by her outburst. "Why, Miss Holden! Whatever has come over you? Would I be wrong to guess that ex-Marshal Custis Long has unfairly turned you against me with his smooth talk and lies?"

"Joe, what do you want?"

"I need to have a long, honest conversation with you about placer gold."

"There isn't any gold to be found on my ranch or even in this county."

He tipped his head to one side and frowned. "That's odd, because your father thought that there was lots of gold hereabouts. He was always prospecting, always panning local streams and looking for it even as he was trying to run your ranch."

"He *never* found gold," Lizzy spat. "Father had a life-long case of gold fever. It cost my mother and me dearly, but even at that he managed to buy and build up our cattle ranch."

Joe Bean raised a finger. "Yes, and that brings up the other thing I need to discuss with you . . . your Lazy H Ranch. We need to talk about it right now."

Lizzy growled. "You and I have nothing more to talk about. Any talking you need to do concerning me or the Lazy H should be with my new partner, Custis Long."

"*Partner*?" Joe asked, his mocking smile fading away to be replaced by a tight-lipped anger.

Lizzy lifted her chin in victory. "That's right! I've deeded over half of the Lazy H to Custis. We're going to be married this summer."

"Congratulations," Joe Bean said, without even trying to sound sincere. "Custis Long would be considered quite a good catch by some women. Whores mostly."

Lizzy's eyes burned. "Get out of this town and county, Joe. That's the best advice I can give you."

"Thanks for the advice, but we still have many things to discuss. I have a room in the same hotel across the street that you and Miss O'Connell are currently sharing. We can talk in private there."

Lizzy started to push past the man. "I'll never speak to you again!"

"Oh, really? Well, before you say anything more, you

need to look up at the hotel room window and wave to my large friend Bert."

Lizzy froze in mid-step. "What?"

"Look," Joe said, pointing up at the Buena Vista Hotel's second-floor windows. "Bert is waving at you from your room. Don't you think it would be good manners to smile and wave back?"

Lizzy didn't want to raise her chin and look up at the window. It took all of her willpower to do so and when she did, she saw a red-bearded giant standing in the window gleefully waving a long bowie knife that glinted in the morning sunshine.

The air went out of Lizzy and she nearly fainted. She dropped her packages and started to run across the street and into the Buena Vista Hotel, but Joe Bean stopped her.

"You friend Teresa O'Connell will be just fine. Bert is a very friendly man. Very *affectionate* ... if you get my drift."

Lizzy swung a fist at Joe, who easily caught her hand in his own and nearly crushed it in his grip.

"Let go of me!" she cried, pain shooting up her arm.

"Then behave yourself and come with me to my room where we'll talk over a few matters of mutual interest. If we can reach an agreement, your friend and my friend Bert will all part on friendly terms. But if not . . ."

Lizzy struggled to free herself and raged, "You're a fiend!"

"I'm a determined man who always gets what he wants, and right now I want you to come to my room and discuss business matters."

Lizzy glanced back up at the window to see the huge, ugly man smiling and picking his yellow horse teeth with the bowie knife. She suddenly realized that Joe Bean was now holding all the cards in this deadly game and that she had no choice but to do as he wanted. Otherwise, Teresa was as good as dead.

"All right," she said. "I'll come with you. But I insist that we leave your door open when I go inside your room."

"Fair enough," he said amicably. "We'll leave it open a crack. After all, you're a lady with property and considered respectable, although that will soon change when people realize that you planned on living with two bachelors out at the Lazy H."

"I don't care what people think!"

"Of course you do," Joe said reasonably. "A beautiful young woman with a fine ranch has to behave with propriety. Otherwise, all the women in town will be snickering and calling you a harlot behind your back."

Lizzy's eyes filled with bitter tears. "If your friend Bert hurts Teresa, I'll . . ."

"You'll do nothing because her fate is entirely in your hands, Lizzy. Now, why don't we continue this conversation in my room with the door slightly ajar for reasons of propriety? This is a very small town and we don't need to start a scandal, do we?"

Lizzy didn't answer as she gathered her packages and marched across the street, with Joe Bean trailing slightly behind and laughing to himself.

"All right," Lizzy said, standing stiffly in the middle of Joe's hotel room with her arms folded across her chest. "Exactly what is it that you *think* we have to discuss?"

"The gold. I still believe you know more than you're telling me. If you tell me where the gold was found by your late father, then we'll go upstairs and tell Bert that he will have to leave your room and Miss O'Connell."

"I've already told you that there isn't any gold!" Lizzy cried in frustration. "How many times do I have to say that!"

Joe studied her intently. "I'm not convinced," he said. "But I have a proposition for you. Tell me where your father struck a vein of gold . . . or sign a deed giving me the Lazy H Ranch."

"Are you crazy!" Lizzy shouted. "I'm not going to sign any such thing!"

Joe shrugged and studiously consulted his pocket watch. "Then in about five minutes, your friend Miss O'Connell is going to find out what it feels like to be repeatedly raped by a pitiless giant."

"No!" Lizzy cried in horror.

"Oh, yes," Joe said, looking pained and resigned. "And here's the worst part. After Bert has done unspeakably filthy acts to that poor young woman, he will gag her and then use that big bowie knife to skin Miss O'Connell alive."

Lizzy launched herself at Joe Bean with such a fury that she actually knocked him back against the wall and got in a hard punch to his right eye. Recovering quickly, Joe balled his fist and struck her in the stomach, bending Lizzy over and causing her to slump to her knees and vomit the remains of her breakfast.

"You're sure a wildcat," Joe said, walking over to the door and locking it. "Now the question is, are you a smart wildcat, or a stupid one?"

Lizzy raised her head, sick with pain and defeat. "What is that supposed to mean?"

"It means that you and Miss O'Connell can both leave this hotel alive . . . or dead. It all depends on how smart you are. The outcome is in your hands alone, Miss Holden. I have a bill of sale for the Lazy H. I assure you that it has been carefully drawn by the best lawyer in this town and will be witnessed."

"Witnessed by who!"

"Why, Bert, of course. He'll witness it when I go up to your room and tell him not to rape and cut Miss O'Connell's throat because you were smart enough to sign over ownership of your fine little cattle ranch."

Lizzy wiped her mouth clean and managed to push herself to her feet. "I hate you more than I've hated anything in my life," she said with choking bitterness. "And you won't get away with this. Don't think you will for one minute!"

"Oh, yes, I will," Joe Bean said with a confident air. "I've got all the right people behind me . . . paid well, of course. And the deed will have been signed by your own sweet hand."

"You bastard!"

"Come on," Joe said. "There's no need use for ugliness. The newly drafted bill of sale is waiting on my desk to be signed. Time is wasting. Bert is a very impatient man, and you must realize we need to get right up to that room before he loses what little control that he possesses."

"All right! I'll sign."

"I knew you were smart," Joe said, coming over and dragging Lizzy to her feet, then leading her to a desk and chair.

"Sit down, Miss Holden, and I'll show you where to sign the bill of sale. It requires you to sign the document three times. Let's begin here on the bottom of page one."

Lizzy's eyes dropped to the legal document. "I'm getting twelve thousand dollars?"

"Not really," Joe said. "Just between the two of us, I'll give you one silver dollar. But twelve thousand is what it says on the bill of sale, and that seemed like a very generous and believable price."

"Not for the Lazy H, it isn't."

"Doesn't really matter, does it?"

"I suppose not," Lizzy said, picking up the pen and signing her name on the first page. "This will never stand up in a court of law. And don't forget, I sold half the ranch to Custis Long."

"No, you didn't," Joe said confidently. "I already checked at the land office and they have no record of any such transaction. The truth is, Miss Holden, that you are . . . I mean were . . . sole owner. Now, here we go to page two, which you need to sign at the bottom."

Tears began to fall on the bill of sale, and that angered Joe Bean enough to make him snatch the document away and gently dab it dry. "Just one more signature and this is over," he said, turning to the final page.

Lizzy signed it.

"Excellent! Now we can go up and see if Miss O'Connell is still alive or not. I think we ought to hurry, don't you?"

Lizzy had nothing more to say, so she let Joe Bean escort her out of the room while praying that the ugly red beast upstairs had not already started raping poor Teresa.

Chapter 15

Longarm had gotten up very early in the dark to make strong coffee and a hearty breakfast. By the time the sun came up, Jesse was stirring and waiting for the coffee to boil.

"Well," the cowboy said, stretching and yawning. "Today you learn how to brand cattle."

"Whoopee," Longarm said sarcastically.

"It ain't so bad," Jesse assured him. "We've only got twenty head to do and we should be done by noon. I'll be on horseback ropin' and draggin' them over to the branding fire. All you have to do is get 'em on the ground and slap the hot iron to them."

"Some of those cattle you found out there running wild on the ranch are pretty good-sized," Longarm said. "I sure don't see how I'm going to throw a five- or six-hundred-pound cow to the ground and hold it while I burn a brand in its hide."

"I'll rope the bigger ones around the hind legs and then you just run up and knock 'em over. It's easy!"

"We'll see," Longarm told him with plenty of doubt in his mind.

"If you're gonna be a rancher, you gotta learn how to do

127

this right," Jesse told him, pouring them both cups of coffee. "And the time to learn is now . . . before Lizzy and Teresa are here to watch and die laughing."

Longarm shot Jesse a hard look that stifled the cowboy's own laugh. "Finish your coffee and let's get this over with."

An hour later, Longarm was standing before a small fire, and the rusty Lazy H branding iron was red-hot at one end. He signaled Jesse, who was riding the roan, indicating that he should bring in the first of the calves they'd be branding this morning.

Jesse was a joy to watch on horseback. He rode with such ease and skill that Longarm thought the tall young man had probably been born on a horse. Jesse put the roan into a gallop, and his loop began to swing as he moved into the restless herd. One quick toss and his loop settled over a calf's head. It was bawling for its mother and fighting the rope, but Jesse and the roan didn't seem to notice as they dragged the fighting calf toward the fire.

"All right!" Jesse called. "Grab this little feller by the neck and by his flank, then use your knee to lift him up and slam him down. You do it right and you'll knock the wind and the fight out of him right away, making the branding that much easier."

Longarm waded in with grim determination. The calf saw him coming and took off past the roan. When it hit the end of Jesse's rope, it somersaulted. Stunned, it lay panting on the ground.

"Grab the iron and put it to him!" Jesse called enthusiastically. "You got to strike while the iron is hot!"

"I've heard that before," Longarm said, grabbing the long handle of the branding iron and feeling its heat even through a pair of thick leather gloves, then running toward the still-stunned and prostrate calf.

"Jump on his neck and put the iron to his hide!"

Longarm did as he was told, and he was appalled at how the iron burned through hair, then raw flesh. The stench was sickening and the calf suddenly came alive and went crazy with pain. It fought off Longarm and scrambled bawling to its feet.

"Dang it, Boss! You got to hold the iron to his hide for a few more seconds. We'll have to do it to the little fella all over again."

"Shit!"

Longarm went after the wild-eyed calf, and it took him nearly five exasperating minutes to finish the job. By the time he was done, he was breathing hard and covered with dirt and calf shit.

"Good work!" Jesse called from the roan. "Now take off my loop and I'll bring you another!"

And so it went for the next three hours . . . only things got even worse when they moved to the bigger, full-grown cows. When they did that, Jesse had to rope each animal's hind legs, then jerk it down and jump off his horse and help Longarm slap the Lazy H brand on its hide. And once, when a cow slung its snotty head and gored Longarm in the butt, it hurt so bad that he thought he'd call it quits. If this was the life of a working cattleman, then he intended to go back to Denver and beg for his badge.

"Just walk it off," Jesse said, clearly enjoying every minute of this ordeal. "Walk it off, Boss. We still got five more cows to go!"

Longarm was in considerable pain limping around rubbing his ass. That sure wasn't getting him any relief, so he just gritted his teeth and said, "Rope another and let's get this Gawdamn miserable job over with!"

They had two cows left to go, and were bent over one insane, thrashing beast, when Longarm happened to look up and see Joe Bean and a big, redheaded man on horseback watching with amused interest.

Longarm's eyes stung with perspiration and his hands

were thickly covered with grime and crap. To make matters worse, their guns and holsters were hanging off a fence post some thirty feet away.

"Hello there, Custis, how do you like the cowboy life!" Joe Bean called with a rifle resting on his saddle horn.

Longarm and Jesse forgot about the fighting cow as the searing branding iron dropped to the dirt.

"What are you doing here?" Longarm demanded, straightening his aching back and butt.

"I come to thank you and your young cowboy friend for branding my cattle and fixing my place up this past couple of weeks."

"What are you talking about?"

Joe Bean shrugged as if what he was about to say was everyday common knowledge. "I own the Lazy H. Its land, cattle, and buildings. I own it all."

"The hell you do!" Jesse shouted, starting to move toward his own six-gun hanging beside Longarm's weapon.

"Don't do that," Joe Bean warned, the barrel of his rifle leveling on the irate cowboy. "If you try to grab that pistol, I'll have to shoot you down and then probably Custis as well."

Longarm jumped forward and grabbed Jesse by the back of his belt. "Don't do it," he warned. "Joe means what he says and he doesn't miss what he shoots at."

"But . . ."

"Don't do it," Longarm growled. "This isn't the time or the place to get ourselves killed."

"Smart," Joe Bean said. "You really ought to listen to him more, cowboy. Might be that you'd live to a fine old age."

When Jesse stopped trying to move forward, Longarm released his belt and said, "What the hell are you doing here, Joe?"

"Like I said, I bought the Lazy H from Miss Holden in

Buena Vista yesterday. I even have a copy of the bill of sale, if you'd care to take a look at it."

"She'd never sell this ranch!" Longarm snapped.

"Oh, but she did," Joe Bean assured him. "And the sale has been dutifully and legally recorded in Salida. But I knew you'd want to see a copy of the sale with Miss Holden's signature in three places."

"You're damn right I do," Longarm said, still not believing what he was hearing.

Joe Bean kept his rifle loosely trained on them both while he reached into his inside coat pocket and extracted the bill of sale. He said, "Come over here nice and easy and I'll give it to you. And remember that I know about that derringer attached to your watch fob."

Longarm did as he was told because there was no choice. He took the document and read it quickly, noting Miss Holden's signature and recognizing it as being valid because he'd read a letter from her only yesterday.

"Well?" Joe Bean said. "I'm afraid you're both fired."

"What did you do to her?"

"Miss Holden?"

"Yeah!"

"She's in Salida and is still in good health. She's waiting for you there along with that other woman. Miss Teresa O'Connell, I believe is her name. A couple of handsome women they are. Real prime stuff."

Jesse's face flushed with anger. "What did you do to Teresa?"

Joe Bean took a peek over his shoulder at the red-haired giant, who smirked. "Bert here took good care of Miss O'Connell. She can tell you all about him when you see her in Salida."

Jesse's face contorted with rage. He glared at Bert and hissed, "If you so much as touched her, I'll kill you!"

Bert's smirk died and his face became a mask of ugliness.

131

"I ain't worried about you, cowboy. I eat men like you every day for breakfast."

"Well, you'll be swallowing lead the next time you swallow, you overgrown ape!"

"Control your boy," Joe Bean warned. "If you want him to live long enough to get on his horse and ride off my ranch, then get him under control or I will shoot him in the guts."

"You do that and you're a dead man," Longarm warned.

"Big talk for an unarmed man coated with dirt and cow shit," Joe Bean answered with a thin smile. "Now give me back that copy and get on your horses and get off my land!"

"It ain't your Gawdamn land!" Jesse shouted.

"Bert," Joe Bean said, "why don't you get off that horse and teach this smart-mouthed cowboy some manners?"

"No!" Longarm said as the huge man started to dismount. "That won't be necessary. We're leaving."

"I can whip up on that big pile of shit!" Jesse yelled. "Let me kick the crap out of him right here and now!"

"No," Longarm repeated, his voice flat and hard. "Not now. Later maybe, but not now."

"Boss!" Jesse pleaded.

"Don't you see that Joe Bean wants you to fight that man? Even if you somehow managed to beat him, Joe would shoot you dead. So get back on the roan, Jesse, and let's get out of here. *Now!*"

Even through his red-hot anger, Jesse heard the message and understood that Longarm knew that to fight was to die. So he swallowed the gorge in his throat and all the pride in his being and whirled around to stomp off to get his cow pony.

"He's a hothead," Joe Bean dryly observed, looking at Jesse swing up into the saddle. "He won't last."

"He'll last," Longarm said. "I'll see to that."

"The cowboy will get you both killed before this is over."

"No one lives forever," Longarm answered, heading for his own horse. "I'm riding back to the ranch to pick up my personal belongings."

"No, you're not," Joe Bean countered, cocking back the hammer of the rifle. "You're leaving with nothing. I'll send whatever belongings you two have at the house into Salida tomorrow. But today . . . right now . . . you've got a choice to live with what you're carrying . . . or die."

Longarm took a glance at his and Jesse's six-guns hanging on the fence post. He was furious that he'd been so careless as to leave them out of reach, but he hadn't wanted to foul the pistols up with dirt or cow shit, so he said, "See you later, Joe."

Joe watched Longarm mount his sorrel and start to rein away. "Oh, Custis?"

Longarm drew up his horse and twisted around in his saddle. "Yeah?"

"You had damn well better remember that you no longer have the protection or authority of a United States marshal's badge. When you resigned, you became just another dead-broke citizen . . . nothing more . . . nothing less."

"I can handle you without a badge," Longarm said.

"We'll see. But you should also know that I have enlisted the help and support of the local law officers in Salida. That means that they are working on *my* side and will stand between us should you or the cowboy decide to take matters into your own hands."

"You paid off the local lawmen?"

Joe Bean laughed. "Let's just say that they know I'll help make their lives a little more comfortable and that they understand who butters their bread. Understood?"

"Understood."

"Custis, as one old friend to another, I'll say that the

best thing for you to do is to collect those two women in Salida and leave this part of the country. To fail to do so could get not only yourself killed, but also put the lives of those two lovely ladies in jeopardy. Understood?"

Longarm was so furious that the best he could do under the circumstances was just to jerk his head up and down and then put spurs to his sorrel and gallop away yelling, "Come on, Jesse!"

Jesse was swearing and cussing a blue streak, but to his credit he was just smart enough to follow orders.

Chapter 16

Longarm and Jesse had few words to exchange as they rode to Salida. When they entered the town, Jesse said, "Hell, we aren't going to stand for them taking the Lazy H and all our belongings, are we?"

"No," Longarm assured the young cowboy. "We sure as hell aren't. But the first thing we need to do is to get our facts straight and make sure that Lizzy and Teresa are safe. After we do that, we talk to the local marshal and the judge and see if Joe Bean really has bought and paid for their support."

"Do you doubt it?"

"Not really," Longarm said. "Joe is smart and he's got enough money to grease the palms of the locals. He's the kind that not only would have bribed them, but he'd also have made it clear that they would be dead men if they do a double cross."

"Yeah," Jesse said. "I can see that he'd do a thing like that. So by giving them cash and then Joe telling them he'd kill them if they betrayed him, he's sorta wrapped up the whole ball of wax."

"I'm afraid that's about how it is," Longarm said. "But it

still won't hurt to lay our cards on the table with the town marshal and judge and tell them that, if they play Joe Bean's game, they're bound to lose sooner or later."

"Tough sell since you don't carry a badge anymore," Jesse observed.

"Yeah, the same thought occurred to me."

"Let's find the women," Jesse said.

It took only a few minutes to find Lizzy and Teresa, who were renting a modest room at the Antelope Hotel. When Longarm saw Lizzy, she looked as if she had aged ten years and she came rushing into his arms sobbing uncontrollably.

"Custis, he made me sign over our ranch! I signed over everything!"

Longarm held Lizzy tight for a few minutes while she cried herself out. Jesse Horn went over and sat on the bed beside an equally distraught Teresa O'Connell. From the look on Jesse's face, Longarm could tell that the young cowboy was beyond rage.

"All right," Longarm said when everyone had settled down. "I want to hear exactly what happened in Buena Vista when you had to sign over the Lazy H."

Lizzy told Longarm and Jesse every detail about how she had gone out to get supplies and how Bert had gone up to their room and how Joe had made it clear that Bert would rape and murder Teresa if the documents were not signed. And how the bill of sale would say he'd paid her twelve thousand dollars when he'd actually only paid Lizzy one silver dollar.

"And who witnessed the signings?"

"That awful man named Bert," Lizzy said, eyes blazing. "I could see in his eyes that he would do terrible things to Teresa if I didn't sign over the ranch."

"No other witnesses?"

"No," Lizzy said. "Everything happened so fast. Once the documents were signed, Joe Bean and Bert disappeared.

136

Fortunately, I have cash enough to carry us awhile, but I lost the ranch, Custis!"

Lizzy burst into fresh tears and Jesse shouted, "Custis, let's get rifles and ammunition and go back out to the Lazy H and kill those two bastards."

"We might do that," Longarm said. "But I'd like to have the law on our side."

"Why!" Jesse shouted. "We know that Bean has paid off the local authorities."

"I still want to talk to them first," Longarm insisted. "We'll get Lizzy and Teresa to swear that they were threatened with rape and death. That Lizzy had no choice but to sign that bill of sale."

"I'll go with you to find the judge and marshal," Jesse Horn said. "I want to see their faces when they start lying to us."

"No," Longarm told him. "I think that it would be better if you stayed here with Teresa. Lizzy, I'd like you to come with me."

"Of course. I can't wait to tell my side of the story."

Longarm took Lizzy's arm and headed for the door. "Lock the door and don't let anyone inside besides myself or Lizzy."

"Don't worry about that," Jesse promised, stretching out on the bed beside Teresa and taking her hand.

Longarm found Salida's marshal, Wade Dunston, dozing in his office chair. He kicked the man's chair leg hard enough to send Dunston sprawling on the floor. The marshal jumped up red-faced and fighting mad.

"What the hell did you do that for!" demanded the small, unkempt man with rumpled clothes and a two-day growth of scraggly beard.

"Because I want you to know that I'm a serious person," Longarm replied. "And that you have even more to fear from me than from Joe Bean."

"What the hell are you talking about?" Dunston's eyes slid to Lizzy, then back to the menacing big man standing a foot taller than himself.

"This is Miss Lizzy Holden. She and her father owned the Lazy H Ranch."

"I know Miss Holden," the marshal said. "How are you doin' today, miss?"

"Not good," she said. "Not good at all. But you already know that, don't you."

The marshal put on his best look of confusion. "What . . . what are you talking about, miss?"

"Yesterday in the Buena Vista Hotel, Joe Bean forced me to sign over my ranch lock, stock, and barrel."

Dunston's eyebrows raised in question. "Oh? I didn't know the Lazy H was for sale."

"It wasn't and it isn't!" Lizzy snapped. "I was forced to sell the ranch and sign a bill of sale. The sales price says twelve thousand dollars, but Mr. Bean only paid me a dollar. And to make it very clear, the Lazy H wasn't for sale at any price."

Marshal Dunston wasn't much of an actor, but he was trying his damnedest to look confused and surprised. "Let me get this straight, you're saying you were forced at gunpoint to sell Mr. Bean your ranch?"

"Not at gunpoint. But Joe Bean had my friend Teresa O'Connell threatened by a man named Bert. Joe Bean warned that, if I didn't sign a bill of sale he had prepared, he would let Bert rape Miss O'Connell, then skin her alive."

"Did you go to the marshal in Buena Vista and tell him all about this?"

Lizzy's fists balled at her sides. "Dammit, Marshal Dunston, you know darned good and well that Buena Vista doesn't have a marshal. Their last marshal was shot and buried more than a month ago and they haven't been able to come up with a replacement."

"Oh, yeah, I think I heard about that." Dunston shook

his head. "Are there any witnesses that would testify that you were forced to sign over your ranch?"

"No."

Dunston threw up his hands and let them fall helplessly at his sides. "Then without witnesses, what am I supposed to do? I don't have any jurisdiction over what may or may not have happened in Buena Vista. I'm just an underpaid local town marshal."

Longarm took a step closer to the man. "You know something, Dunston, that's almost word for word what I expected you to say."

"Well, what else could I say? And who the hell are you anyway?"

"Marshal . . . no, I'm ex-Marshal Custis Long. And I'm also the half-owner of the Lazy H."

Dunston looked over at Lizzy. "That a fact?"

"It is."

"Any papers putting his name as co-owner on a deed for the Lazy H Ranch?"

"We were planning on doing that soon after arriving here in Salida," Lizzy said. "But Joe Bean forced me to sign over the ranch before we even could get to the county seat."

"Humph," Dunston said. "Well, is this new deed recorded in Joe Bean's name?"

"I'm sure it was. Joe Bean is no dummy. It would have been the first thing he'd have done when he arrived here in your town."

"You ought to check with the county recorder on that. It could be Joe Bean forgot," Dunston suggested, as if this would be helpful and get these people out of his office.

"We're going to see the local judge now," Longarm said. "We're going to tell him what happened and ask him to swear out a warrant for Joe Bean and Bert's arrest. Then we'll come back here and I expect you to go out to the Lazy H and arrest those two men."

"What!" Dunston actually paled.

139

"You heard me," Longarm said. "You're going to arrest Joe Bean and his hired thug Bert."

"On what charges?"

"How about grand larceny and assault?"

Dunston scratched his head. "*What* assault?"

Lizzy swallowed hard. "While he was up in my hotel room, Bert did something to Miss O'Connell. He knocked her out and . . ."

"And what?" Dunston asked eagerly.

Lizzy colored. "When Teresa was barely conscious, Bert did things to her that are quite unspeakable."

Dunston was suddenly very interested. "Did he rape her when she was knocked out cold?" he asked, unable to hide his excitement.

"No!" Lizzy took a deep breath. "Bert put his fingers where they should never have gone."

Dunston's little undershot jaw dropped. "Holy cow! He finger-fucked her?"

Longarm's hand shot out, and he grabbed Dunston by the front of his shirt and shoved him over the top of his desk. "You sick, sorry little excuse for a lawman! Bert did something that only a pervert would do to a helpless woman. And you're going to arrest him for that or I'm going to beat you to a bloody pulp and then put you in a pine box!"

"But I . . . I can't!"

"Why not?"

"Because this Bert fella is sure to deny it. And unless there was a witness . . . same thing as there is no witness other than Bert to Miss Holden's signing away her ranch . . . why, there's just no evidence to make an arrest."

"We'll go see the judge now," Longarm said, feeling as if he could not stand being in this man's presence for another second without choking him to death. "And when we come back, dammit, we'll expect your help!"

Dunston turned away when Longarm and Lizzy

stomped out of his office. And after they were gone, he started emptying his desk and gathering his personal belongings. He'd gotten well paid by Joe Bean, but not paid well enough to defy an enraged Custis Long.

It was, Dunston decided, time to get out of town and quit a winner.

Chapter 17

Dusk had fallen when Custis and Lizzy stood on the wide veranda of a stately Victorian home where Judge Elford B. Smedley resided. "Is Judge Smedley a reasonable man?" Longarm asked before knocking.

"The judge is old and crotchety, but he did like to play checkers with my father."

"Well, I'm not in the mood to play checkers," Longarm said. "Is Smedley honest or corruptible?"

"The latter, I'm afraid. Elford has always put Elford before the letter of the law, but he does have a few good qualities. He's smart and well-read in the law and in most cases fair . . . unless it comes to putting a little money in his own pocket."

"Do you think it is likely Joe Bean has already bribed the judge?"

"I'm afraid that is probably the case," Lizzy said. "Judge Smedley arrived in Salida about ten years ago with nothing but the clothes on his back and thanks to the bribes, he now owns this fine Victorian home and a good many of the businesses in town."

Longarm shook his head with disgust. "There's nothing

143

worse than a crooked judge. How do you think it best to handle this one?"

Lizzy considered the question for a moment. "I know for certain that Elford Smedley is not going to be intimidated by you or anyone else like Marshal Dunston. If you threaten the judge physically, he'll slam the door on us, go find a shotgun, and try to kill you."

"All right, then what approach shall we take?"

"We can't appeal to his fairness," Lizzy decided. "Not if Joe Bean has already paid him cash."

"What then?"

Lizzy thought a moment, then said, "Custis, Judge Smedley has sent a lot of men to the gallows and a good deal more to prison. If you could convince him that *he* will be sent to prison if he doesn't cooperate with us, that would make him tremble with fear. Also, since his god is money, we could try to use that against him."

Longarm didn't understand. "What do you mean?"

"I mean," Lizzy said, "we should try to find out how much Joe Bean paid the man and offer more."

But Longarm shook his head emphatically. "No! It's against my principles to pay bribe money."

"Well, if that is the only way we can get the Lazy H Ranch back in our names, then it isn't against *my* principles," Lizzy said. "And I'd appreciate it if you didn't stand in my way of offering Smedley a bribe bigger than the one he's gotten from Bean."

"Let's try to do it my way first. If that fails, you can try to outbid Joe Bean, although I think it's wrong."

"Right or wrong, I want the Lazy H back!"

"I understand." Longarm knocked on the door and after a few minutes, a black maid answered the door. She was in her fifties, a substantial woman who peered at them through the crack in the door.

"That you, Miss Holden?"

"It is, Iris. Could we please see the judge? It's very important."

"I'm afraid that the judge is not well today. You'll have to come back and maybe he will see you tomorrow."

"Iris, you know I wouldn't bother the judge after hours if this wasn't very important."

"Yes, Miss Holden, but . . ."

"Give him this," Lizzy said, extending five dollars. "And here's a dollar for your trouble."

Iris grinned. "I guess the judge might get up to see you folks for a few minutes. Please come sit inside the parlor. Can I tell him who your gentleman friend is, Miss Holden?"

"Mr. Custis Long."

"Yes, ma'am. Mr. Custis Long. Why he's a fine, tall, strappin' sort of a man, Miss Lizzy. You and Mr. Long sweet on each other?"

"We are," Lizzy said, looking a little embarrassed. "Now please go tell the judge we only need to see him for a few minutes in the parlor."

"You wantin' the judge to marry you two tonight, Miss Lizzy?"

"No," Lizzy answered. "Not tonight. Maybe this summer, though."

"That sure be fine, you two gettin' hitched, Miss Lizzy. He is a big, handsome galoot!"

"Yes, he is," Lizzy said, now almost laughing despite their dire circumstances. "Please go ask the judge if he will meet with us in his parlor for a few minutes."

"You two come right on inside and wait there. The judge, he'll see you for sure," she said, slipping the money in her dress pocket and hurrying away.

When they were alone for a moment, Longarm leaned close to Lizzy and said, "You even have to bribe the *maid*?"

"Of course," Lizzy said. "Iris likes money every bit as much as the judge. It's common knowledge that Iris has quite a savings account in our bank and a whole lot more money stashed away in the judge's house or backyard."

"Unbelievable," Longarm said. "Simply unbelievable."

"It's how it works here," Lizzy said. "Just remember that there are only two things Judge Smedley will fear . . . imprisonment and loss of his money."

"I'll keep that in mind," Longarm said, almost eager to meet this old money-grubbing scoundrel.

They waited about five minutes, and then they heard a poking sound on the steps leading down from the upstairs bedrooms. A few minutes later, Judge Smedley appeared in the door way of the parlor using a hickory cane with a silver handle. Elford Smedley was a tall, cadaverous man probably in his late sixties, and he wore a smoking jacket and pajama bottoms and fur-lined moccasins. He was a little stooped, but he had a full mane of silver hair and a long white goatee. All in all, Smedley had an unmistakable authority and presence about him that Longarm knew would give him stature in any frontier courthouse.

"Well, well," the judge said with arms outstretched toward Lizzy. "How good to see you again."

"You too, Judge. This is my friend Mr. Custis Long."

"Would he also be known as Longarm?"

"Sometimes I've been called that," Longarm said with characteristic modesty. "For quite some time I've been the long arm of the law."

"Yes, I've heard a good deal about you. But I take it you are no longer a United States marshal?"

"No, I'm not, sir."

"But I can tell by your manners and bearing that you are a gentleman born and raised," the judge said with a keen eye and a smile. "Is this man your new boyfriend, Lizzy?"

146

"Custis saved my life in Denver where we met and became attached. He and I intend to be married this summer and restore the Lazy H."

"How nice," the judge said in a way that held no conceit and made Longarm wonder what the judge really knew about Joe Bean and his swindle involving the Lazy H. "How very nice indeed."

"Judge, could we have a few words with you?" Longarm asked.

"That's why I'm standing here. But first, whiskey anyone?"

"I'd enjoy a glass," Longarm said.

"Me, too," Lizzy added.

"Then that makes three of us," the judge said, looking pleased. "Let's all have a seat and Iris will serve us."

The judge shouted for Iris in a surprisingly strong voice, and when she appeared, he told her to pour them three tumblers of his finest whiskey.

"Yes, sir," she said. "Ain't Mr. Long a handsome fella, though, Judge? You can tell they sweet on each other. Gonna get married this summer!"

"Yes, so they have informed me."

When the drinks were distributed all around, Judge Smedley dismissed Iris, who obviously did not want miss out on the ensuing conversation. Longarm noticed the tops of the money still in her dress pocket as she left the parlor. He figured the judge had gotten little if any of the bribe. Maybe he'd recently gotten enough bribe money from that damned Joe Bean to pad his pockets for a good long while.

"What can I do for you tonight?" the judge asked after they'd sipped their whiskey and offered compliments as to its quality.

"Judge," Lizzy began, choosing each word with great care, "I want you to know how much my father and I have always liked and respected you."

"Well, thank you very much," Smedley replied, for the first time looking a bit uncomfortable. "And I had a great deal of admiration for your father. He wasn't quite my match at checkers, but he would give me a go of it most of the time. I miss him."

"Me, too," Lizzy said. "And now I want to tell you what happened to me in Buena Vista at the hands of a terrible killer named Joe Bean and his brutish accomplice Bert."

Smedley's smile melted and his eyes narrowed. "Lizzy, before you begin, I should tell you that I have recently had some dealings with Mr. Bean and he has told me that he bought your ranch for twelve thousand dollars . . . which seems to me a fair price."

"But he didn't buy it! Judge, Joe Bean *stole* my Lazy H Ranch! He forced me to sign a bill of sale and then he gave me a silver dollar . . . his sick idea of a joke. He and this Bert have taken my ranch and all that I own!"

The judge listened with his bony fingers steepled on his lap. "That's quite an accusation, Lizzy. Can you prove what you're saying?"

"No," she said, crestfallen. "But you must know that I would never sell the Lazy H Ranch. Never!"

The judge swirled the whiskey in his glass for a moment, and then sipped it with obvious enjoyment. "Lizzy, you have been away from these parts for many years. Mr. Bean told me that he had purchased the ranch and recorded the new deed in our county courthouse. I admit that I was surprised and a bit saddened that the Lazy H was no longer owned by you. But times change and so do priorities and properties, so I accepted the fact and gave no further thought to the matter."

"Judge Smedley, I'm telling you that I was *forced* to sign that bill of sale or else Bean and his friend Bert would have killed Teresa O'Connell in Buena Vista."

"I've never heard of the woman. But would this Miss

O'Connell be willing to testify that she was being held against her will and that this Bert fellow would have killed her?"

"Of course she would."

"And that she saw you sign the bill of sale under extreme duress?"

Lizzy blinked. "Why, Judge, Miss O'Connell couldn't do that because she was clinging to consciousness on the bed."

The judge frowned and got up to refill his glass. "Lizzy, I'm afraid that, if this O'Connell woman didn't see you being forced to sign the bill of sale, I can't help you."

"But she was assaulted in our hotel room!"

"In Buena Vista?"

"Yes!"

"Then of course you should go back to Buena Vista and report the crime and then see the judge who presides there. Let me see. His name is Oliver Morton. Judge Oliver Morton will listen to what you have to say and . . ."

"Judge, I want my ranch back and I'm sure that Judge Morton won't do a thing to help me," Lizzy said in exasperation.

Smedley tossed down his whiskey and pushed himself unsteadily to his feet. "You have just put me in a very unpleasant frame of mind, Lizzy. I don't like to be upset before my bedtime because it fouls up my sleep. Furthermore, you come here making this claim without any proof whatsoever of the fact that you were coerced into signing that bill of sale and that you were not paid the fair price for your ranch of twelve thousand dollars."

"I don't have anything like that kind of sale money! At most, I have a few thousand dollars, and that all came from the sale of my livestock."

The judge shrugged his narrow shoulders. "In court, even a slow-witted attorney would say that you could have stashed the twelve thousand dollars away where it couldn't be found."

"But . . ."

The judge was getting upset and he was starting to leave the room, but paused and turned back to say, "Listen to me, my dear young woman. You have to bring me proof of what you say. Without proof, I cannot possibly help you or your friend here in any way."

Longarm could see that Lizzy had played the honesty card and they'd failed to win the game. Now it was his turn to speak and attempt to make this judge change his mind and his attitude.

"Judge Smedley," he said, "before coming here I was a deputy United States marshal for many years out of Denver."

"Yes, but what . . ."

"I know *all* the judges on the State Supreme Court. They know me well and trust that I would never lie to them."

Smedley stiffened. "And your point?"

"My point is that Joe Bean stole the Lazy H Ranch and I'm going to find a way to prove it . . . no matter what it takes. And I'm also going to draft a long letter to the presiding judge of the State Supreme Court detailing the circumstances and telling him that our plea for simple justice has fallen on your very deaf ears here in Salida."

"How dare you!"

"Furthermore," Longarm said, cutting off the judge's outburst, "I'm going to poke around Salida and get evidence that you have been taking bribes for years."

"That's preposterous!" Smedley slammed his cane down on the floor. "Slanderous!"

"Oh, is *it*?" Longarm said, his voice turning hard and cold. "I don't think I'll have any trouble finding people who will be glad to tell me about how you've feathered your own nest over and over again. And here's the best part, Judge Smedley."

"I'm finished listening to your groundless accusations. Leave this house at once!"

But Longarm stood his ground. "Judge, I'm going to see that you are sent to the state prison and that restitution is made to all those who had to pay you for your judicial decisions."

Smedley's old hand shot out and grabbed the door to keep him from toppling over. "You . . . you . . . sonofabitch."

"I'll see that you go to prison and lose everything you've got," Longarm added, almost starting to enjoy himself. "Doubt me on that and you'll soon be wearing stripes because you have no idea of the influential contacts I have made in Denver over the same years when you were lining your own pockets with local bribes."

"Lies! All lies!"

"We'll see, Judge. I don't think I'll have any trouble finding people to testify as to your dishonesty on the bench."

All at once, Smedley seemed to cave in on himself. He faltered, and Lizzy eased him back into his parlor chair. "Would you care for another whiskey, Judge?"

His bony hand fluttered across his ashen face. "Yes, if you please, my dear. Thank you."

Lizzy refilled all of their glasses. Judge Smedley now looked old and frightened half to death.

"Judge," Longarm said after a long silence. "I think we need to rethink this bill of sale that Lizzy was forced to sign against her free will. Don't you?"

"Yes," he whispered.

"I couldn't hear you, Judge. Could you speak a little louder? Don't you think we can find a way to show that Lizzy was coerced into signing that bill of sale and that the document is invalid?"

"I . . . I'm sure that we can find some way to prove that," the old man said, his voice a little stronger as he quickly emptied his glass. "But Mr. Bean is a very . . . very determined and dangerous man. If I . . ."

"I'll try to protect you," Longarm promised. "But you can't take any more bribes or I will inform the State Supreme Court of your illegal activity, and that would not only deprive you of your livelihood, but also of your name and reputation."

"I don't want that. Please. I'm too old to start over again."

"Of course you are," Longarm said gently. "And that's why you're going to help us right a great wrong."

"Yes, I'll help you."

"Good," Longarm said, tossing down his whiskey. "We'll be back tomorrow morning. You look very tired tonight, Judge. I think you should get Iris to help you up to your bedroom and then try to get some sleep."

"I won't be able to sleep tonight," he said with quiet certainty.

"Perhaps tomorrow night," Longarm told him, taking a stunned Lizzy by the arm and heading for the front door.

Outside, she stopped him on the porch and said, "You might have caused Judge Smedley's old heart to burst in there just now."

Longarm nodded. "Yeah, I might have. But you tried to do it by approaching the injustice the right way and the judge wasn't going to help us. So that left me no choice but to play rough."

"You sure do know how to do that."

"The stakes are high, Lizzy. We either get your ranch back and put Joe Bean in prison, or we walk away with nothing and let a wrong go unpunished. Which way would you have it go?"

"Our way."

"That's what I thought," Longarm said, taking her back to the hotel and thinking about some serious lovemaking.

Chapter 18

Longarm and Lizzy spent the next few days quietly talking to the town's businessmen and citizens. The problem was that no one dared to speak out against Judge Elford B. Smedley because he was the ultimate law in Salida and a very powerful individual. However, Longarm finally met a man who had plenty to say about the crooked judge.

"I owned by far the best livery stable in Salida," the burly and bitter man whose name was Thomas Kincaid said. "It was handed down to me by my father, and I worked hard to build the business up until I was making a good living for myself, the wife, and my three kids. The judge could see that I was making good money and he wanted to buy my business and then have me manage it for him."

"And you said no," Longarm guessed.

"That's right," Kincaid said. "Why would I want to manage something that my father and I had built from scratch? Besides, the judge was only offering two thousand dollars for the barns, corrals, wagons, and a very nice stone house my family has lived in for years."

"When you turned Smedley down, did he get angry?"

"He got furious with me!" Kincaid exclaimed. "The

judge said I was too stupid to realize that he was offering me far more than my business was worth. When I said I didn't care how much it was worth because it wasn't for sale and never would be for sale, the judge got even madder and told me that I'd be sorry someday soon."

Longarm could guess what had happened, but he felt the need to ask. "So what happened?"

"The judge was right. It all started one day when Judge Smedley and one of his hired men rented my buckboard and then had a terrible wreck a few miles outside of town."

"A wreck?" Longarm asked.

"Yes," Kincaid said bitterly. "The judge said that the two rented horses pulling the buckboard spooked and ran over the side of the road north of town, causing the buckboard to flip and damn near killing the judge."

"So they lost control of your rental horses?"

"That's right. And Judge Smedley had to be carried into his house. He lay in bed for a week, claiming that his spleen had been ruptured and that he was pissing blood and lying on death's doorstep."

Longarm raised his eyebrows. "Pissing blood?"

"Yeah, lots of it, too," Kincaid replied. "The judge even got old Doc Patterson to come by with a bottle of bloody piss just to prove the point to me and anyone else who would listen. But I believe they put some tomato juice in the piss so it only *looked* bloody. Anyway, the judge was said to have nearly died. When he recovered, he sued me for grave physical damages saying I was at fault for renting him bad, runaway horses."

"Had your team ever spooked or run away before?" Longarm asked.

"Hell, no! They were as tame as a pair of old milk goats! They'd never have run over the side of the road. But there it was . . . my carriage was wrecked, one of the horses had to be put down, and on top of that the judge sues me for eight thousand dollars for pain and suffering."

"Did anyone else see the wreck besides the judge and the hired man?"

"No, of course not." Kincaid's expression was desolate. "I would bet anything that the judge got off the buckboard before his hired man whipped that team into a run and then forced them off the road. Of course the buckboard flipped! The hired man jumped and he didn't suffer a scratch."

"What's his name?"

"Pete Gordon."

"Is Gordon still around?" Longarm asked.

"Oh, yeah. He's the new manager of my stable!"

"So the judge sued and you lost everything you'd ever worked for."

"Of course I did!" Kincaid said, face twisted with rage. "I not only lost the stable, but also my home. Gordon lives in it now with some hussy and he manages the stable, while me, the wife, and my kids live in a crummy rented shack out at the end of town and I try to find work whenever and wherever I can just to put scraps on our table."

"Did the judge rule in his own favor?" Longarm asked, looking for evidence against Smedley.

"Oh, no. He's way too smart for that. He had his friend, Judge Oliver Morton, come over from Buena Vista and listen to the testimony. Of course, with Morton and Smedley both being crooks, the judgment was made in Smedley's favor. Since I didn't have even close to eight thousand dollars, the judge made a big show of telling everyone he would show me mercy and just take my home and business and all my livestock and wagons."

Longarm could see the pain and the anger in this wronged man, and he laid a hand on Kincaid's shoulder and said, "I'll have a talk with the judge's hired man, Pete Gordon. He was there when the buckboard flipped and so he knows that the accident was rigged."

"Sure he knows! But now he's got a fine house, a regular paycheck, and feels real important. There is no way that

Gordon is going to tell you the truth and double-cross the judge who owns the livery he now manages."

"Is Pete Gordon a tough man?"

"Yeah," Kincaid said, "I'm afraid that he is. I wanted to go over and wring his neck forcing him to tell the truth, but my wife talked me out of it because Gordon is fast and deadly with either a gun or a knife. My wife said it was better to be broke and without a home than to be dead. I would never admit this to her, but sometimes I think that she's wrong in my case."

"Her advice was sound," Longarm told the former livery owner. "Let me get Pete Gordon to tell the truth."

"Even if you could do that, who would listen?" Kincaid asked. "Judge Smedley? Marshal Dunston? Who would listen and help me?"

"*I* will," Longarm promised. "And I have important friends who would overrule Judge Smedley and send him straight to prison."

Kincaid's face grew very earnest. "Are you being honest with me?"

"I am and I'm going to prove it by getting Pete Gordon to tell me the truth and then write it down and sign it as fact."

"If you can do that . . ." Tears welled up in Kincaid's eyes, and he roughly brushed them dry with his tattered sleeve while he struggled to find his voice. "If you could do that, I'd owe you . . ."

"You'd owe me nothing," Longarm assured the man. "And for the record, I want to hang Judge Smedley as bad as you because he helped Joe Bean swindle Miss Lizzy Holden out of the Lazy H Ranch."

"So I heard."

Longarm headed up the street for the stable that was recently owned and then lost by Thomas Kincaid.

"Howdy, mister, can I help you with a horse or buggy this fine day?" asked a well-dressed man sitting on a log smoking a corncob pipe. "My name is Pete Gordon and I manage this stable."

Longarm's eyes shuttered. "You do?"

Gordon was in his thirties, a dandy obviously full of his newfound self-importance. He was wearing a fancy gun on his hip, which in itself was suspicious since that was not a common thing that a stable man would wear day in and day out.

"Yes, sir. I am the chief dog . . . whatever you want to call it. Now, what can I help you with today?"

"The truth for starters," Longarm said, seeing Gordon's grin sag a little. "I want you to tell me the truth about what happened the day that you and judge went out and wrecked Mr. Kincaid's buckboard."

"What the hell are you talking about?" Gordon jumped to his feet, clamping his jaw down tight on the stem of his corncob pipe. Gone was the friendliness that had been there only moments before, replaced by distrust and dislike.

"People call me Longarm."

Gordon blinked and then cleared his throat. "Uh . . . yes, I've heard plenty about you."

Longarm didn't bother to tell Gordon that he had recently resigned as a federal officer of the law. "Then you know that when I ask a man for the truth, he'd damn sure better tell me the truth."

Now the dandy looked very nervous. "I don't have anything to say to you, Longarm."

"Oh, yes, you do," Longarm said, starting toward Gordon, who began to back away in fear until he was pressed up against his barn wall.

"Don't come any closer!" Gordon warned, hand dropping toward his sidearm.

But Longarm kept advancing and when Pete Gordon finally made a stab for his six-gun, Longarm was close enough to punch him with a sledgehammer right hand, slamming Gordon's head back against the barn. The man's

157

eyes rolled up in his head, and Longarm followed up the overhand right with a vicious left uppercut into Gordon's solar plexus that bent him over gasping and retching.

"Please, no more," Gordon choked, fighting for air.

Longarm grabbed the man before he toppled into the dust, and then he hauled him around behind the barn where they could not be seen from the street. "All right, Gordon, we both know that the buckboard wreck was a setup. Tell me all about it or I'll make you wish you'd never been born!"

"If I do that, the judge will . . ."

"Forget about Smedley!" Longarm roared, cocking back his big fist. "If you don't tell me the truth right now, you'll not live long enough to have to worry about Smedley or anyone else in this world. I'll beat you to death and claim that you were stomped by those rental horses."

"All right! All right! Judge Smedley set it all up. I did the driving and jumped off the buckboard just before it went over the side of the road and down an embankment."

"And the bloody piss in the bottle!"

"Ketchup and water!"

Longarm stared at Gordon with hard, merciless eyes. "We're going to Mr. Kincaid's house and you're going to write a confession saying exactly what you've just told me."

"No, please. Smedley will have me killed by Joe Bean!"

"Judge Smedley will be locked up in prison by the time he knows what hit him," Longarm promised. "And Joe Bean is at the top of my list to handle."

Pete Gordon, still pale and fighting for breath, allowed himself to be pushed and shoved into the stone house that he'd taken from Thomas Kincaid. After Longarm had a written and signed statement from the frightened man, he said to Gordon, "Don't say a word to anyone about this."

"Hell, no!" Gordon exclaimed. "Will you get the judge locked up before you tell him I turned on him?"

"Yeah," Longarm said. "And you won't be the only one in this town that will tell me true stories about how the judge has feathered his own nest here in Salida these past ten years. When I'm done collecting statements, the judge will have so many counts of fraud and corruption leveled against him that he'll get a life sentence."

"I'll lose this job and it's the best deal I ever had," Gordon whined. "I'll go back to working for nothing again."

"That's your problem," Longarm said without a trace of sympathy. "You knew what you and the judge were doing when you swindled Mr. Kincaid and his family out of their home and business. And I doubt either one of you lost a minute of sleep over it."

Gordon's chin dropped. "I'm ashamed."

"You ought to be," Longarm told the man. "But at least you're alive. I could have shot you dead out there a few minutes ago. I would have shot you dead if I hadn't needed you to write out this statement and sign it."

Gordon sighed deeply. "I'm going to leave Salida tonight."

"No, you're not," Longarm told him. "You're going to stick around until I tell you that you can leave, and that won't be until you see an *honest* judge."

"Will he send me to prison?"

"I don't know," Longarm said. "But if you tell it straight and I think you're truly repentant, I'll recommend leniency."

"I am repentant!"

"No, you're scared and you should be," Longarm said, folding up Gordon's written statement and leaving with a bad taste in his mouth.

Chapter 19

"I got a signed statement from a man named Pete Gordon saying that Judge Smedley used him to cheat Thomas Kincaid out of his livery," Longarm announced. "Now that we've got one man to cooperate, others will quickly follow."

"What do you want us to do?" Lizzy asked.

"I want to help, too," Teresa blurted. "I'm plenty capable of moving now and I want to do whatever I can."

"All right," Longarm told the two women. "Start going around Salida and asking people about Judge Elford Smedley. Tell them that we have a statement sworn out by one local businessman that the judge has broken the law for his own personal gain. Tell whoever will listen that you're getting other sworn statements and that a federal judge from Denver is on his way right now to Salida to make sure that wrongs are righted and justice is finally served."

"Is a federal judge really on his way here?" Lizzy asked.

"No," Longarm admitted. "But I'm going to write my ex-boss, United States Marshal Billy Vail, and tell him what we're up against and the mountain of evidence that we're getting against both Joe Bean and Judge Smedley. I'm going to ask Billy Vail to send a federal judge here immediately."

"Will he do that even though you quit just before you left Denver?" Jesse asked.

"I don't know," Longarm answered. "But it's worth a try and we might as well run the bluff. If we can get enough embittered people like Thomas Kincaid to step forward and tell their stories, the game is over for the judge and Joe Bean."

"If either man finds out what you're doing," Jesse said, "they'll come at us with everything they have. I'm told the judge knows every gunfighter and back-shooter in Colorado and he's got the money to hire them all."

"I realize that," Longarm said. "That's why we have to always be on our toes and watch each other's back."

"What can I do?" Jesse asked.

"There's not much you can do except to help me protect Lizzy and Teresa. I'm hoping that sooner or later either Joe or his dumb giant Bert will come into Salida for supplies."

"And then?" Lizzy asked.

"Then I force the play," Longarm told them. "I tell either Joe or the giant that we're gathering evidence against them."

"If you do that, won't Joe Bean go for his gun?" Lizzy asked.

"I expect he will," Longarm said. "And if I beat him, half of the problem is eliminated."

Lizzy swallowed. "But . . ."

"I'll be all right if it's a fair showdown," Longarm said, trying to sound confident. "I'm younger and probably faster than Joe is now. Joe has been living hard since he handed over his badge some years ago. He's bound to be slower than he once was with a gun."

"But what if he isn't!" Lizzy exclaimed. "Surely, you can think of some better way to . . ."

Longarm cut off her protesting words with gentle fingers pressed to her lips. "Lizzy," he explained, "I know Joe Bean and he won't go down without a fight. He simply is

162

not going to throw up his hands and surrender to be sent to the gallows."

Lizzy wrapped her arms around Longarm's neck. "I just don't want you to be killed," she whispered in his ear.

"Not likely to happen," he replied, although he knew that Joe Bean was as deadly a man as he'd ever face.

"Why don't we just ambush the sonofabitch and be done with it?" Jesse suggested. "I'll do it."

"No!" Longarm softened his voice. "It's one thing to arrest a man, it's another to murder him. I won't be a part of murder and neither will you."

"Just a thought," Jesse said. "And it sure would solve all the problems. With Bean dead, the judge would lose his strongest ally. It would all come down on the judge's head and he'd be finished in Salida."

"Let me do this my way," Longarm said. "Okay?"

"Okay."

"All right, then. If you ladies want to go out and try to get some people to start telling you how the judge has been swindling everyone and taking bribes, go do it. Just don't tell anyone that it was Pete Gordon who first signed a statement to that effect. If the word gets out that it was Gordon, he's as good as dead and no help to us in a courtroom."

"Maybe he deserves to die," Jesse offered.

"He might, but we need him to testify to that federal judge that I'm hoping will be sent right away from Denver," Longarm told the young cowboy.

Longarm was sitting on a chair in front of their hotel later that afternoon having a smoke and chatting with Jesse when a huge man on a big horse rode into town.

"My, oh, my!" Longarm said, tipping his hat down lower on his face. "Don't look, but guess who just rode into town for supplies?"

"Is it Bert?"

"That's right. I knew that sooner or later one or the

163

other would have to come in for liquor and food, and I was hoping it would be the big man. Tip your hat down, Jesse. I don't want Bert to recognize us until we've got him where we want him."

"And where is that?"

"Coming out of the mercantile carrying supplies in both hands."

"I see."

Jesse and Longarm watched the giant dismount in front of the mercantile and then glance up and down Salida's main street. Satisfied that no one was paying him any attention, Bert went inside the store to make his purchases.

"Let's give him a few minutes," Longarm suggested. "When he comes out of the store, we'll jump him."

"Then what?"

"Then we make him a believer."

Jesse frowned with confusion. "A believer in *what*?"

"You'll see."

Longarm soon finished his cigar, and then he came to his feet and checked his gun. Jesse did the same.

"Here we go," Longarm said, starting across the street to confront Bert. "Just hang back and let me make the play. Jump in only if something goes wrong."

"Like what?"

"Like if Bert gets his hands around my neck and starts to wring it like I was a live chicken."

"Okay."

There were several chairs lined up in front of the mercantile, and Longarm took the one nearest to the door where Bert would exit.

"Here he comes," Longarm said about ten minutes later. "Just hold steady."

"I am steady," Jesse replied.

Longarm let Bert walk out of the store, and then he stepped up behind the giant with his gun in his hand and jammed it into Bert's spine, saying, "Keep moving, Bert, or I'll plant a pill in your backbone that will make you into a turnip."

Bert *wasn't* smart. Instead of doing as Longarm ordered, the giant tried to pivot and swing a sack of food at Longarm. But Bert was slow and ponderous, so Longarm simply smashed him across the back of the skull with the barrel of his gun. Bert's skull, however, was so thick that the giant actually stayed on his feet and managed to grab Longarm by the throat.

Unwilling to shoot the big man and unable to match his incredible strength, Longarm croaked, "Jesse, help!"

The young cowboy jumped out of his chair and pistol-whipped Bert a second time across the forehead with all of his strength. This time the giant's eyes rolled up into his head and he collapsed on the boardwalk, spilling groceries and bottles in all directions.

"Shit," Longarm wheezed, massaging his throat and knowing he was very lucky that the big man hadn't used both of his massive hands. "Jesse, let's get him into the alley."

The cowboy didn't understand. "Why the alley?"

"Because I don't want the whole damn town to watch what is going to happen next," Longarm answered. "You take that arm, I'll grab this one, and we'll drag him."

"Be like dragging a draft horse."

"I know. Let's just get it done," Longarm growled.

He and Jesse grunted with the effort it took to drag the giant around into the nearest alley and then lay him out cold.

"He's bleeding pretty good from both wounds in his skull," Jesse observed.

Longarm massaged his constricted throat and wheezed. "He'll live. Go find a big can or bucket and fill it with water, then dump it in Bert's face."

"You gonna tie his hands and feet up before we do that?" Jesse asked.

"Might be a good idea," Longarm said, his voice sounding funny from the violent squeeze it had just suffered. "Find some rope or wire and we'll do that before we douse his face with water."

"Anything else I can do while you just stand here wheezing?" Jesse asked with sarcasm.

"Nope."

"Lucky I was there to crack his thick skull a second time," Jesse said as he was leaving.

"Yeah, it was. Thanks!" Longarm croaked.

"Don't mention it. After what that sonofabitch did to my Teresa in Buena Vista, it was a pleasure. I only wish I'd have killed him."

"I'm glad that you didn't, Jesse. Now get that rope and bring some water."

A few minutes later, they had the giant hog-tied, and then they pitched a bucket of water into his ugly, blood-streaked face. Bert came awake, roaring and fighting his bonds, but he was helpless.

"What the hell!" the giant shouted. "Untie me and I'll kill you both!"

"You're going to hang before you can do that, big man."

Bert stopped struggling and gaped at Longarm. "What do you mean?"

"I mean that unless you are willing to tell the truth about how Joe Bean murdered Lizzy Holden's father and how you would have killed Miss O'Connell, you're going to hang even if it takes a *chain* to do it instead of a stout rope."

"No!"

"Yes," Longarm said with certainty. "We know that you were in on everything, and you're going to sign a sworn statement that you helped swindle Miss Holden out of her ranch for Joe Bean. And if you don't, I'll make sure that the hangman botches his job and you strangle."

All Bert's fight was now replaced by sheer terror. "No, please. I saw a bad hanging a couple of years ago in New Mexico. I saw a man's face go purple and swell up like a huge melon. His tongue got bigger than a dill pickle and it stuck out and his eyes . . . Oh, Gawd, no!"

Longarm was merciless. "You're gonna suffer the exact same fate if you don't cooperate and testify against Joe Bean."

"He'll kill me, but at least it will be quick," Bert said, looking as if he had just received his death sentence.

"I'll keep you alive and make sure that Joe never kills or cheats anyone again," Longarm promised.

"You could do that?"

"I can do that," Longarm told the giant. "But only if you cooperate."

"I'll do it," Bert said without hesitation. "Just kill Joe as quick as you can or he'll kill me first."

"Agreed."

"Okay," Bert said. "So long as I don't hang and just get sent to prison."

Jesse pushed forward. "You violated Miss O'Connell, you overgrown sonofabitch! If you don't hang, I'll kill you myself!"

Longarm pushed in front of the cowboy to keep him away from Bert. "Jesse!"

"I will," Jesse raged. "Teresa could feel what he'd done to her up in that hotel room. This sonofabitch deserves to be strangled by a rope!"

Longarm could see that the young cowboy was going to snap and probably draw his gun and empty it into Bert, so he disarmed Jesse and shoved him away from the man.

"If you kill Bert, Lizzy might never get her ranch back. Bert is the *only* one that can say what really happened in Buena Vista that day that the bill of sale was signed. Don't do this to Lizzy."

Jesse shook like a wet dog, but in the end he nodded. "All right. Bert lives. But he'd better get life in prison or someday I'll by Gawd give Teresa her due justice!"

"Fine," Longarm said. "Just help me get a signed statement out of Bert and then put him in jail."

"And then what?"

"We go arrest Joe Bean out at the Lazy H," Longarm told the cowboy. "And I'll need your help."

"You've got it," Jesse said, eyes still a little crazy with wanting to kill Bert. "You've got it."

"Good," Longarm said. "Now get ahold of yourself and let's get Bert to a desk with paper and pen."

"On your feet," Longarm ordered Bert.

"I can't stand with my ankles tied!"

"Cut his ankles free," Longarm told Jesse.

Jesse drew his knife and held it to Bert's face. "If you don't do exactly as you're told and this doesn't work out, so help me, Gawd, I'll cut you into pieces so small that even a Gawddamned ant wouldn't choke on 'em!"

Had the situation been less grim and tense, Longarm would have laughed.

Chapter 20

They were surprised when they took Bert to the marshal's office and discovered that Dunston had fled Salida without a word to anyone. The jail key was hanging on a peg and the office was cluttered and unkempt.

"So what are we going to do now?" Jesse asked. "We can't just lock Bert up and leave him here alone. Someone who knows him might come in and set him free."

Longarm thought about that problem a moment and said, "Let's put him in the cell and then ask Lizzy and Teresa to take turns watching over him while we go out to the Lazy H Ranch and arrest Joe Bean."

"Or kill him."

"Or kill him," Longarm agreed. "And I'm afraid that's what we'll have to do once Joe figures his game is up and he's lost the ranch and is going to the gallows for murder."

They shoved the bloodied giant into the cell and locked the door. Bert grabbed the bars and shook them in anger and frustration. Longarm saw that the bars were loose and he said, "Bert, if you try to pull out the bars and escape, I will hunt you down like a dog and make sure that you hang at the end of a logging chain. But if you stay here and behave yourself, I promise I'll ask the federal judge to show you leniency."

"I ain't goin' no place," Bert muttered. "Just keep Joe Bean and the judge away from me."

"We'll do that," Longarm promised. "And you'll be guarded by Miss O'Connell and Miss Holden."

"That ain't too comforting," Bert said with sarcasm. "Unless they want to come in here and give me some lovin'."

Filled with rage, Jesse leapt at the cell bars, but Bert stepped back and laughed in his face. "What's the matter, cowboy? You want to leave that gun of yours out there and join me? You want to get your neck wrung and your face beat to a pulp today?"

Jesse's knuckles were white on the bars. "I'm not afraid of you."

"You should be," Bert said, licking his lips. "I'd kill you with my bare hands and laugh while I was doin' it."

Longarm pulled the young cowboy back from the cell. "He's just trying to get your goat, Jesse. Let him be."

"I wish I could put a bullet in his sick little brain right now!"

"Well, don't." Longarm found pen and paper on Dunston's desk. In just a few minutes and with some prompting from Bert, he scribbled out a confession stating what Bert and Joe Bean had done to steal the Lazy H Ranch from Lizzy. Satisfied that he had a good account of the matter, Longarm read it aloud to Bert and then extended it through the bars.

Bert couldn't read, but he could sign his name. "I could tear this paper up and you'd have nothin'," he bragged, watching Longarm closely to see if the threat would give him any advantage.

"If you do that, I'd write another, and then I'd have to come into that cell with a gun and either shoot you to death or get you to sign. So why don't we just cut out the crap and

170

you sign the damned confession and then I'll keep my word and try to cut you a good deal with the federal judge."

Bert considered his complete lack of options and finally nodded. "All right. Give it to me and I'll sign the damned thing."

Once the confession was signed, Longarm breathed a sigh of relief. Now Lizzy was assured of getting her beloved Lazy H Ranch back.

"Jesse, go find our women and tell them to come and watch over the prisoner until we return with Joe Bean either dead or alive."

"Sure thing, Boss."

A half hour later, Longarm and Jesse saddled their horses and left for the Lazy H Ranch armed to the teeth and expecting a fight. Teresa and Lizzy wished them farewell, and Lizzy said, "Shoot Joe Bean on sight, Custis. Because from what you've told me about the man, that's what he'll try to do to you and Jesse."

"I know," Longarm replied. "But even though I don't wear a lawman's badge anymore, I still can't bring myself to ambush a man."

"Be careful!" Teresa called to Jesse. "And hurry back to me!"

"I will," the cowboy vowed as he touched his spurs to the flanks of his roan and led off at a gallop down Salida's main street.

Lizzy and Teresa waved good-bye and headed for the marshal's office.

"Seeing that horrible man again isn't going to be easy," Teresa said, her nerves raw.

"You don't have to do this," Lizzy told her. "I can stay with Bert until Custis and Jesse return with Joe Bean while you rest at the hotel."

"No, I can do this."

"I hope they bring Joe Bean back draped across a saddle,"

Lizzy said through clenched teeth. "He killed my father thinking there was gold to be found on our ranch, then he tricked me when I hired him, and finally he swindled me out of the Lazy H."

"It's all in the past," Teresa said. "Custis sent a letter to his boss in Denver asking for a federal judge. When the judge comes and makes things right by putting Smedley forever behind bars, this evil will pass."

"I know. And Salida will be relieved of a long, ongoing nightmare."

They went into the marshal's office and gave Bert a cup of water for what he claimed was a raging thirst. Never a man to be satisfied by small kindnesses, Bert said, "How about some food? I ain't eaten nothin' since last night."

Lizzy and Teresa exchanged glances. Lizzy said, "He should be fed. We don't know how long it will be before Custis and Jesse return."

"No, but . . ."

Lizzy said, "Teresa, I noticed that you're limping badly. You've been on your feet too much while we've gotten others to swear to the fact that Judge Smedley has been taking bribes."

"I'll be all right. I'm just tired."

"You're really hurting," Lizzy said. "And you look exhausted."

"Well," Teresa said with a half smile as she settled into Dunston's chair, "Jesse and I made love last night and into the wee hours of this morning. We had . . . well, quite a time together."

Lizzy shook her head. "So did Custis and I, but I'm not the one on the mend after being shot. Maybe you and Jesse ought to . . ."

"Hey!" Bert shouted. "You women want to cut out the bullshit and go find me something to eat! I told you I'm starving in here."

Lizzy flushed with anger. "You look like you could

starve for a month and still be hog fat. But I'll go find you something to eat and you'd better behave yourself with Miss O'Connell. If you give her even a little grief, so help me you will starve and not get so much as a drop of water. Do we understand each other, Bert?"

He nodded, but his smile did not die.

As soon as Lizzy hurried off to get their prisoner food, Bert called, "Hey, Teresa, I'll bet you remember me putting my finger inside you up in that hotel room. You were tight and juicy, girl! I should have used you when I had the chance instead of listening to Joe down there in the street. I could have done it and no one but you and I would have known."

"Shut up!" Teresa screamed, clamping her hands over her ears and going to the far end of the office with her eyes squeezed tightly shut.

"I should have humped the hell out of you, girl! Maybe if I had, you'd remember what a big cock I have and you'd want some more right now!"

Bert laughed hysterically.

Teresa screamed at the man and dashed for the door, hearing Bert's ribald and hysterical laughter follow her like a ghost. She ran down the boardwalk until she came to an open space with a big tree, where she collapsed and burst into tears.

After a few minutes, Teresa roughly scrubbed the tears away and squared her shoulders. "I've got to go back and watch that animal until help arrives," she said to herself. "Lizzy will be back with food soon. Then Jesse will come back, too. I've *got* to do my part."

Teresa composed herself and brushed dirt off her skirt. Scrubbing the last of the tears away, she hurried back up the street to the marshal's office.

When she went inside, she froze dead in her tracks because Judge Elford B. Smedley was standing beside the cell with the keys in his hand preparing to free Bert.

"Stop that!" Teresa shouted, her voice breaking.

The judge, caught by surprise, whirled around and then calmly said. "Why, you must be poor Miss Teresa O'Connell. I've heard all about you, mostly from Bert."

"Judge, please put those keys back on the desk and leave right now," Teresa told the old man in a voice that shook so badly, she hardly recognized as her own. "You *shouldn't* be here!"

"Oh?" he asked mildly. "Well, neither should any of us. Dear young lady, this man has been illegally jailed and being the judge of this town, I have a sworn duty to set him free."

"No!" Teresa saw a rifle and shotgun resting in a wall rack close by. She was not accustomed to using firearms, but she had shot a few times, and now the only thing that she could do was to make a try to grab the shotgun in order to stop the judge from setting Bert free.

"Miss O'Connell," the judge said, his voice calm and resonate. "I'm going to release Bert now and . . ."

"You can't do that!" Teresa cried, edging toward the rifle rack.

"But first I want to know where that signed confession he was forced to make is to be found." Judge Smedley's eyes shifted away from her for an instant. "Is it in that office desk?"

Teresa's mind was whirling. "Uh . . . uh, yes!"

"Good," the judge said, stepping away from the cell and starting toward the desk. "It was a forced confession and so it isn't really worth the paper it's written on. I must take possession of it."

Using his fancy cane, Judge Smedley hobbled over to Dunston's desk. He opened the top drawer and rummaged through its contents. "Not in this drawer," he said, glancing up at Teresa. "Maybe the next?"

"Maybe," Teresa said. When the judge looked back

down at the desk and pulled open the next drawer, Teresa lunged for the gun rack and grabbed the shotgun.

"Judge, watch out!" Bert cried from behind the bars.

Judge Smedley was always well armed and although he was old, he was still very skilled with weapons. In a smooth and often practiced motion, he brought a .32-caliber pistol out from under his black frock coat.

Teresa raised the shotgun she prayed was loaded. She was so afraid that the barrel of the shotgun waved back and forth. Pointing the shotgun at the judge and Bert directly behind him, she pulled the trigger even as she felt the inside of her head explode like a firebomb.

Chapter 21

"That's far enough!" Joe Bean shouted from the ranch house's front porch. "What do you want, Custis!"

"You're under arrest for the murder of Mr. Holden and for swindling his daughter out of this ranch. Joe, the game is over and you've lost!"

"You're no longer a lawman! You don't have any authority to arrest me. Go away and I'll let you and that cowboy live."

"Come out here with your hands over your head, Joe. Come out and we'll let a judge and jury decide your fate."

Bean actually barked a laugh. "If it's to be Judge Smedley, I might just agree."

"It won't be, Joe. I've sent for a federal judge out of Denver."

Joe's chin dropped to his chest and he thought about that a minute.

Longarm interrupted the man's thoughts. "Bert has given me a sworn statement about how you killed Mr. Holden and what he did to Teresa O'Connell in Buena Vista forcing the fraudulent sale of the Lazy H."

Joe Bean's head jerked up and his body stiffened. "You

made Bert talk and sign a confession? I don't believe it because that dumb ox is illiterate!"

"Wrong!" Longarm yelled. "I wrote the confession, but Bert can sign his own name *and he did.* It's over and you're done here. Now surrender peacefully and take your chances with a federal judge."

"No, thanks!" Joe shouted, jumping into the ranch house and then reappearing an instant later with a rifle in his fists.

"Jesse, let's get out of his range!"

"I thought we *were* out of his range!"

"Not quite!" Longarm said, spurring his sorrel into a hard run with the cowboy and the roan racing at his side.

Three rifle shots cut through the air and Jesse's hat sailed off his head. It made the young cowboy ride even lower and spur harder.

When they were finally out of rifle range even for a man like Joe Bean, Longarm drew up on the reins and took cover behind a low hill.

"What now?" Jesse asked.

"We get our rifles, flank the house, and go after him," Longarm said. "Just remember one thing, Jesse. This man is a marksman and he's a better shot than you or me."

"Thanks for building my confidence," Jesse said, tying his horse and pulling out his Winchester. "Maybe it would be better to wait until after dark."

"No," Longarm said. "Joe Bean would find a way to escape past us and go on the run."

"Okay, then," Jesse said. "Let's flank the bastard and kill him."

Longarm nodded grimly and headed around behind a hillock to the south. Jesse hit the ground and began to crawl to the north whispering, "Let's just make damn good and sure we don't mistakenly shoot each other."

"Good point," Longarm said in full agreement.

Fifteen minutes later and without another shot having been fired, Longarm figured he was in a good position to make a run for the house. He could see across the ranch yard to where Jesse had taken up position, and he signaled for Jesse to start shooting.

The cowboy opened fire at the front door of the ranch house, and Longarm could see wooden splinters flying. Then, totally unexpectedly, Joe Bean jumped out of the back door and sprinted toward the hay barn, scattering a flock of barnyard chickens who had been scratching for seeds and insects.

Longarm threw his rifle to his shoulder, put his eye on the line of the barrel, and began firing at Joe. He missed two hurried shots, and thought he'd missed a third until Joe staggered and fell to the dirt just twenty feet from the barn.

Longarm jumped up and ran toward the downed killer, dropping his rifle and drawing his pistol.

"Custis, he's faking it and still alive!" Jesse shouted as he came racing toward the downed outlaw.

Joe Bean's gun was coming up and he was going to take a quick aim and kill Longarm, but when Jesse yelled, he was momentarily distracted and twisted around toward the cowboy.

That momentary hesitation cost Joe Bean his life. Longarm and Jesse both opened fire on the downed killer, and their bullets chewed Joe Bean apart as he lay jerking this way and that in the dirt and chicken shit.

Chapter 22

Everyone said it was the finest burial that Salida had seen for many years. The whole town was there when the minister said his final sorrowful words over the brave young woman that few had known but whose story would be retold again and again over the years in central Colorado.

"I'll never have another like her," Jesse said, his face streaked with tears and ravaged with grief. "Teresa was brave, funny, loving . . . she was everything a man could ever want in a woman, and now she'll never even see California."

Longarm's head was also bowed in grief. He briefly glanced up at the other two fresh graves, and found a small measure of satisfaction that Judge Smedley would never again cheat anyone or take his dirty bribe money. The only one that had attended the judge's funeral was his housemaid, Iris. After a very brief sermon over the judge, the big black woman had then shown everyone who would listen the last will and testament that the judge had supposedly signed and executed, leaving her his Victorian mansion with a free and clear title. No one knew who would end up with Smedley's ill-gotten business properties, but Longarm figured that would all be sorted out fairly in the weeks and months that would follow.

As for Bert . . . nobody had known his last name and hadn't cared, so his grave didn't even have benefit of a headstone or simple wooden marker. Bert had been a vicious nobody and no one would remember his passing, much less grieve over it.

"Teresa died fighting," Lizzy told the grief-stricken young cowboy at her side. "She died giving her life to make sure that justice was served."

Longarm nodded in agreement. "There are other Judge Smedleys out there and Joe Beans as well. Lizzy, I'm going to ask for my badge back. I just can't be a rancher and let evil men triumph over good men."

She was wearing a black, see-through lace veil. "Custis, there are *other* lawmen."

"I know. But I have to be and do what I am," Longarm quietly explained. "And what I am is a lawman, not a rancher or cowboy."

Lizzy drew back her veil, "But . . ."

Longarm kissed Lizzy on both cheeks. "Jesse Horn promised to stay and help you rebuild the Lazy H. He can do that better than I ever could."

"But it's half yours!"

"No," Longarm said quietly. "It never was and it never will be."

Lizzy reached out to Longarm, shaking her head in disagreement. "Custis, please . . ."

"I'm sorry, Lizzy, but I've given a lot of thought to this and my mind is made up. I wouldn't be happy roping and branding cows even if I could learn to do it well. And though you don't see it right now, someday you'll know that my leaving you was the right and only sane thing to do."

Fresh tears ran down Lizzy's cheeks.

Longarm looked over at Jesse Horn. "Take special care of Miss Holden and I know she'll do the same for you."

Jesse managed to nod, his eyes bloodshot and locked on Teresa O'Connell's fresh grave.

182

"So long, cowboy."

"So long, Marshal."

Longarm left the funeral gathering and walked over to his handsome sorrel gelding. He mounted the horse and rode away not daring to look back, fearing he might weaken and change his mind about everything. Trying to convince himself that he'd done the right thing, he said aloud, "They don't see it now, but Lizzy and Jesse are the perfect match. Together, they're gonna build something here that will last for their children and grandchildren."

Longarm pushed the sorrel into an easy trot and headed back toward Denver. He kind of expected he would meet his boss, Billy Vail, and a federal judge hurrying toward Salida. He'd save them from going any farther, and then he'd ask Billy for his badge back and he'd ask the federal judge to swear him back in as a lawman.

Watch for

**LONGARM AND THE
PECOS PROMENADE**

the 360th novel in the exciting LONGARM
series from Jove

Coming in November!

And don't miss

**LONGARM AND THE
VALLEY OF SKULLS**

Longram Giant Edition 2008

Available from Jove in October!

GIANT-SIZED ADVENTURE FROM AVENGING ANGEL LONGARM.

BY TABOR EVANS

2006 Giant Edition:

LONGARM AND THE OUTLAW EMPRESS

2007 Giant Edition:

LONGARM AND THE GOLDEN EAGLE SHOOT-OUT

2008 Giant Edition:

LONGARM AND THE VALLEY OF SKULLS

penguin.com

M240AS0508

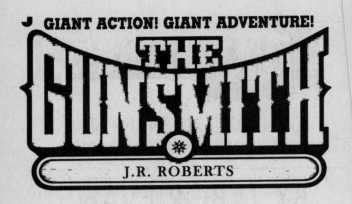

GIANT ACTION! GIANT ADVENTURE!

THE GUNSMITH

J.R. ROBERTS

Little Sureshot And
The Wild West Show
(Gunsmith Giant #9)

Dead Weight
(Gunsmith Giant #10)

Red Mountain
(Gunsmith Giant #11)

The Knights of Misery
(Gunsmith Giant #12)

penguin.com

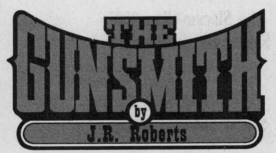